"Don't let the easy accessibility of Maile Meloy's writing fool you; she's capable of witchcraft. . . . These eleven stories are quick, powerful jabs, startling in their economy; you're propelled toward each ending, certain she won't be able to wrap it up in one more page, and you're proved wrong every time." —*Time*

"Though it might seem strange to praise a writer for the things she doesn't do, what really sets Meloy apart is her restraint. She is impressively concise, disciplined in length and scope. And she's balanced in her approach to character, neither blinded by love for her creations, nor abusive toward them. . . . She's such a talented and unpredictable writer that I'm officially joining her fan club; whatever she writes next, I'll gladly read it."
—Curtis Sittenfeld, *The New York Times Book Review*

"Superbly crafted, these hard little tales wind through the ways people fail to relate to each other and even to themselves—their central insight being how complicit we are in creating our own misery. . . . In the best short stories—by Poe, Raymond Carver, Hemingway, Flannery O'Connor, or Alice Munro—there is always malaise, if not outright heartache, on the horizon. In less able hands this convention turns lugubrious and contrived. But Meloy's lean, targeted descriptions and her ultimately compassionate eye make this journey hurt so good." —*Los Angeles Times*

"After two well-received novels, Meloy returns to the short story, the form in which she made her notable debut and to which her lucid style is arrestingly well suited. Many of these stories are set in Meloy's native Montana, and all are about domestic distress—about love, mostly, and the trouble stirred up by its often inconvenient insistence. Several are poised in the limbo of adultery, in the time between act and confession. Always true to her wide-ranging though consistently introspective characters, Meloy convincingly depicts the inchoate emotion that drives people, while also distilling meaning from it."   —*The Atlantic*

"If life is all about choices, as the saying goes, then what happens when we simply can't make up our minds about what's most important? In her second volume of short stories, *Both Ways Is the Only Way I Want It*, acclaimed novelist Maile Meloy (*Liars and Saints, A Family Daughter*), who first stunned critics in 2002 with her debut story collection, *Half in Love*, cracks at our nagging desire to have it all (the answers, the romance, the payout, and, in one case, the late grandmother come back to life) in eleven tightly written, remarkably fluid narratives, most of which unfold in sleepy towns across Meloy's native Montana."   —*Elle*

"Precise and restrained, Meloy's diagnoses of a very American malignancy have an authentic moral force. So does her merciful treatment of the characters in its grip and of the victims of its spread. She has a scope and maturity that at their most rigorous attain the grandeur of prophecy."   —*Slate*

"Maile Meloy's impressive *Both Ways Is the Only Way I Want It* hides no cubic zirconias among diamonds. The stories are all lustrous, the language as pristine as a lake in Montana, where several of them are set. . . . Order or disorder? Cold or warmth? Freedom or safety? Such conflicts converge in a perfect storm of ambivalence, self-justification, and blind hope. Has ever a title been a more perfect match to its content? Meloy's characters want it both ways. . . . We readers, however, get to have it all. We can dip into the collection savoring one delicious morsel at a time or devour the whole book in a single sitting. In the gifted hands of this storyteller, treats abound."   —*The Boston Globe*

"Maile Meloy is a bit of a magician. Her stories move effortlessly, or seem to; that's the trick. In *Both Ways Is the Only Way I Want It*, Meloy's subject is ambivalence. Her characters—small-town, small-time doctors and lawyers, parents and children, husbands and wives—are variously at odds with themselves. One by one, they come up against the precise moment of getting what they want or think they want, only to find themselves immobilized or irresolute or crushed with disappointment, no deliverance in sight."   —*The Cleveland Plain Dealer*

"In a Maile Meloy story, the thrill is in our own perception. Meloy never amplifies or underscores. Her unadorned, low-key prose allows us to come close in to her characters. In such proximity, how terrifyingly aware we become. . . . Meloy's style is disciplined and sly. She keeps a perfect poker face. And we're players in the game."   —*The Dallas Morning News*

"There is one line in Maile Meloy's newest story collection that completely slayed me. . . . And in fact, there are many moments before and after that line that left me awestruck as I wondered how she was able to capture a feeling—typically one that's very familiar, like the flushing embarrassment of an unexpected advance, or the sudden fury found in a bout of sibling rivalry—and create it anew. The effect is both masterful and ephemeral: All of a sudden, it's as if your own life is reflected back to you. This is what great story writers do, and in the stories that follow—whose characters revel or unravel in their relationships to love and family—Meloy pinpoints the ambivalence running through our most powerful emotions, be it love, jealousy, grief, or loneliness. That she writes with so much truth and wisdom and restraint makes *Both Ways Is the Only Way I Want It* an unexpected pleasure."
—*The Louisville Courier-Journal*

"The award-winning Meloy continues to deliver stories that please and surprise as each narrative's small world unfolds. . . . Readers who have waited impatiently for Meloy's return to this genre . . . have a treat in store."
—*Library Journal* (starred review)

"Meloy's great strength as a writer [is] her skill with clarity and control. The images and storylines in *Both Ways Is the Only Way I Want It* are clean, yet complex, and somehow Meloy deftly avoids being too obvious. Her dialogue also earns high marks. But what edges out the other qualities of *Both Ways* is that these stories, even in their simplicity, are so deep and involving that they forbid their readers to stop turning the pages. Not only will you want to read this book in one sitting, you will want to read each story a second time—and a third. . . . [Meloy] is undeniably talented, and *Both Ways* is the latest installment in what is sure to be a long list of beautiful, truthful tales from Maile Meloy."
—*BookPage*

ALSO BY MAILE MELOY

A Family Daughter
Liars and Saints
Half in Love

BOTH WAYS IS
THE ONLY WAY I WANT IT

MAILE MELOY

RIVERHEAD BOOKS

New York

RIVERHEAD BOOKS
Published by the Penguin Group
Penguin Group (USA) Inc.
375 Hudson Street, New York, New York 10014, USA
Penguin Group (Canada), 90 Eglinton Avenue East, Suite 700, Toronto, Ontario M4P 2Y3,
Canada (a division of Pearson Penguin Canada Inc.)
Penguin Books Ltd., 80 Strand, London WC2R 0RL, England
Penguin Group Ireland, 25 St. Stephen's Green, Dublin 2, Ireland
(a division of Penguin Books Ltd.)
Penguin Group (Australia), 250 Camberwell Road, Camberwell, Victoria 3124, Australia
(a division of Pearson Australia Group Pty. Ltd.)
Penguin Books India Pvt. Ltd., 11 Community Centre, Panchsheel Park, New Delhi—110 017,
India
Penguin Group (NZ), 67 Apollo Drive, Rosedale, North Shore 0632, New Zealand
(a division of Pearson New Zealand Ltd.)
Penguin Books (South Africa) (Pty.) Ltd., 24 Sturdee Avenue, Rosebank, Johannesburg 2196,
South Africa

Penguin Books Ltd., Registered Offices: 80 Strand, London WC2R 0RL, England

This is a work of fiction. Names, characters, places, and incidents either are the product of the author's imagination or are used fictitiously, and any resemblance to actual persons, living or dead, business establishments, events, or locales is entirely coincidental. The publisher does not any have any control over and does not assume any responsibility for author or third-party websites or their content.

The following stories have been previously published, in slightly different form:
"Travis, B." (*The New Yorker*), "Red from Green" (*The New Yorker*), "Lovely Rita" (*Playboy*),
"Two-Step" (*Zoetrope: All-Story*), "The Girlfriend" (*Prospect*, UK), "Liliana" (*The Paris Review*),
"Agustín" (*Ploughshares*), "O Tannenbaum" (*Granta*).

Grateful acknowledgment is made to reprint the following:
"Coming Right Up," from *The Really Short Poems of A. R. Ammons* by A. R. Ammons.
Copyright © 1990 by A. R. Ammons. Used by permission of W. W. Norton & Company, Inc.

First Riverhead hardcover edition: July 2009
First Riverhead trade paperback edition: July 2010
Riverhead trade paperback ISBN: 978-1-59448-465-0

The Library of Congress has catalogued the Riverhead hardcover edition as follows:

Meloy, Maile.
   Both ways is the only way I want it / Maile Meloy.
      p.   cm.
   ISBN 978-1-59448-869-6
   1. Family—Fiction.   2. Relationships—Fiction.   3. Psychological fiction.
4. Montana—Fiction.   I. Title.
   PS3613.E46B68   2009   2008050342
   813'.6—dc22

PRINTED IN THE UNITED STATES OF AMERICA

10   9   8   7   6   5   4   3   2   1

FOR GEOFFREY WOLFF

One can't
have it

both ways
and both

ways is
the only

way I
want it.

—A. R. AMMONS

CONTENTS

BOTH WAYS IS

THE ONLY WAY I WANT IT

TRAVIS, B.

CHET MORAN GREW UP in Logan, Montana, at a time when kids weren't supposed to get polio anymore. In Logan, they still did, and he had it before he was two. He recovered, but his right hip never fit in the socket, and his mother always thought he would die young.

When he was fourteen, he started riding spoiled and unbroke horses, to prove to her that he was invincible. They bucked and kicked and piled up on him, again and again. He developed a theory that horses didn't kick or shy because they were wild; they kicked and shied because for millions of years they'd had the instinct to move fast or be lion meat.

"You mean because they're wild," his father had said when Chet advanced this theory.

He couldn't explain, but he thought his father was wrong. He thought there was a difference, and that what people meant when they called a thing "wild" was not what he saw in the green horses at all.

He was small and wiry, but his hip made it hard for him to scramble out from under the horses, and he broke his right kneecap, his right foot, and his left femur before he was eighteen. His father drove him to Great Falls, where the doctors put a steel rod in his good leg from hip to knee. From then on, he walked as though he were turning to himself to ask a question.

His size came from his mother, who was three-quarters Cheyenne; his father was Irish and bullheaded. They had vague dreams of improvement for their sons, but no ideas about how to achieve them. His older brother joined the army. Watching him board an eastbound train, handsome and straight-limbed in his uniform, Chet wondered why God or fate had so favored his brother. Why had the cards been so unevenly dealt?

He left home at twenty and moved up north to the highline. He got a job outside Havre feeding cows through the winter, while the rancher's family lived in town and the kids were in school. Whenever the roads were clear, he rode to the nearest neighbors' for a game of pinochle, but mostly he was snowed in and alone. He had plenty of food, and good TV reception. He had some girlie magazines that he got to know better than he'd ever known an actual person. He spent his twenty-first birthday wearing long johns under two flannel shirts and his winter coat, warming up soup on the stove. He got afraid of himself that winter; he sensed something dangerous that would break free if he kept so much alone.

In the spring, he got a job in Billings, in an office with friendly secretaries and coffee breaks spent talking about rodeos and sports. They liked him there, and offered to send him to the main office in Chicago. He went home to his rented room and walked around on his stiff hip, and guessed he'd be stove up in a wheelchair in three years if he kept sitting around an office. He quit the job and bucked bales all summer, for hardly any money, and the pain went out of his hip, unless he stepped wrong.

That winter, he took another feeding job, outside Glendive, on the North Dakota border. He thought if he went east instead of north, there might not be so much snow. He lived in an insulated room built into the barn, with a TV, a couch, a hot plate, and an icebox, and he fed the cows with a team and sled. He bought some new magazines, in which the girls were strangers to him, and he watched *Starsky and Hutch* and the local news. At night, he could hear the horses moving in their stalls. But he'd been wrong about the snow; by October it had already started. He made it through Christmas, with packages and letters from his mother, but in January he got afraid of himself again. The fear was not particular. It began as a buzzing feeling around his spine, a restlessness without a specific aim.

The rancher had left him a truck, with a headbolt heater on an extension cord, and he warmed it up one night and drove the snowy road into town. The café was open, but he wasn't hungry. The gas pumps stood in an island of bluish light, but the truck's tank was full. He knew no pinochle players here, to help him pass the time. He turned off the main street to loop through town, and he drove by the school. A light was on at a side door and people were leaving their cars in the lot and going inside. He slowed, parked on the street, and watched them. He ran a hand around the steering wheel and tugged at a loose thread on its worn leather grip. Finally he got out of the truck, turned his collar up against the cold, and followed the people inside.

One classroom had its lights on, and the people he had followed were sitting in the too-small desks, saying hello as if they all knew each other. Construction-paper signs and pictures covered the walls, and the cursive alphabet ran along the top of the chalkboard. Most of the people were about his parents' age, though their faces were softer, and they dressed as though they lived in town, in thin shoes and clean bright jackets. He went to the back of the room and took a seat. He left his coat on, a big old sheepskin-lined denim, and he checked his boots to see what he might have dragged in, but they were clean from walking through snow.

"We should have gotten a high school room," one of the men said.

A lady—a girl—stood at the teacher's desk at the front of the room, taking papers from a briefcase. She had curly light-colored hair and wore a gray wool skirt and a blue sweater, and glasses with wire rims. She was thin, and looked tired and nervous. Everyone grew quiet and waited for her to speak.

"I've never done this before," she said. "I'm not sure how to start. Do you want to introduce yourselves?"

"We all know each other," a gray-haired woman said.

"Well, she doesn't," another woman protested.

"You could tell me what you know about school law," the young teacher said.

The adults in the small desks looked at each other. "I don't think we know anything," someone said.

"That's why we're here."

The girl looked helpless for a second and then turned to the chalkboard. Her bottom was a smooth curve in the wool skirt. She wrote "Adult Ed 302" and her name, Beth Travis, and the chalk squeaked on the *h* and the *r*. The men and women in the desks flinched.

"If you hold it straight up," an older woman said, demonstrating with a pencil, "with your thumb along the side, it won't do that."

Beth Travis blushed, and changed her grip, and began to talk about state and federal law as it applied to the public school system. Chet found a pencil in his desk and held it like the woman had said to hold the chalk. He wondered why no one had ever showed him that in his school days.

The class took notes, and he sat in the back and listened. Beth Travis was a lawyer, it seemed. Chet's father told jokes about lawyers, but the lawyers were never girls. The class was full of teachers, who asked things he'd never thought of, about students' rights and parents' rights. He'd never imagined a student had any rights. His mother had grown up in the mission school in St. Xavier, where the Indian kids were beaten for not speaking English, or for no reason. He'd been luckier. An English teacher had once struck him on the head with a dictionary, and a math teacher had splintered a yardstick on his desk. But in general they had been no trouble.

Once, Beth Travis seemed about to ask him something, but one of the teachers raised a hand, and he was saved.

At nine o'clock the class was over, and the teachers thanked Miss Travis and said she'd done well. They talked to each other about going someplace for a beer. He felt he should stay and explain himself, so he stayed in his desk. His hip was starting to stiffen from sitting so long.

Miss Travis packed up her briefcase and put on her puffy red coat, which made her look like a balloon. "Are you staying?" she asked.

"No, ma'am." He levered himself out from behind the desk.

"Are you registered for the class?"

"No, ma'am. I just saw people coming in."

"Are you interested in school law?"

He thought about how to answer that. "I wasn't before tonight."

She looked at her watch, which was thin and gold-colored. "Is there somewhere to get food?" she asked. "I have to drive back to Missoula."

The interstate ran straight across Montana, from the edge of North Dakota, where they were, west through Billings and Bozeman and past Logan, where he had grown up, over the mountains to Missoula, near the Idaho border. "That's an awful long drive," he said.

She shook her head, not in disagreement but in amazement. "I took this job before I finished law school," she said. "I wanted any job, I was so afraid of my loans coming due. I didn't know where Glendive was. It looks like Belgrade, the word does I mean, which is closer to Missoula—I must have gotten them confused. Then I got a real job, and they're letting me do this because they think it's funny. But it took me nine and a half hours to get here. And now I have to drive nine and a half hours back, and I have to work in the morning. I've never done anything so stupid in my life."

"I can show you where the café is," he said.

She looked like she was wondering whether to fear him, and then she nodded. "Okay," she said.

In the parking lot, he was self-conscious about his gait, but she didn't seem to notice. She got into a yellow Datsun and followed his truck to the café on the main drag. He guessed she could have found it herself, but he wanted more time with her. He went in and sat opposite her in a booth. She ordered coffee and a turkey sandwich and a brownie sundae, and asked the waitress to bring it all at once. He didn't want anything. The waitress left, and Beth Travis took off her glasses and set them on the table. She rubbed her eyes until they were red.

"Did you grow up here?" she asked. "Do you know those teachers?"

"No, ma'am."

She put her glasses back on. "I'm only twenty-five," she said. "Don't call me that."

He didn't say anything. She was three years older than he was. Her hair in the overhead light was the color of honey. She wasn't wearing any rings.

"Did you tell me how you ended up in that class?" she asked.

"I just saw people going in."

She studied him and seemed to wonder again if she should be afraid. But the room was bright, and he tried to look harmless. He was harmless, he was pretty sure. Being with someone helped—he didn't feel so wound up and restless.

"Did I make a fool of myself?" she asked.

"No."

"Are you going to come back?"

"When's it next?"

"Thursday," she said. "Every Tuesday and Thursday for nine weeks. Oh, God." She put her hands over her eyes again. "What have I done?"

He tried to think how he could help her. He had to stay with the cows, and driving to pick her up in Missoula didn't make any sense. It was so far away, and they'd just have to drive back again.

"I'm not signed up," he finally said.

She shrugged. "They're not going to check."

Her food came, and she started on the sandwich.

"I don't even know school law," she said. "I'll have to learn enough to teach every time." She wiped a spot of mustard from her chin. "Where do you work?"

"Out on the Hayden ranch, feeding cattle. It's just a winter job."

"Do you want the other half of this sandwich?"

He shook his head, and she pushed the plate aside and took a bite of the melting sundae.

"I'd show you if you could stay longer," he said.

"Show me what?"

"The ranch," he said. "The cows."

"I have to get back," she said. "I have to work in the morning."

"Sure," he said.

She checked her watch. "Jesus, it's quarter to ten." She took a few quick bites of sundae and finished her coffee. "I have to go."

He watched as the low lights of the Datsun disappeared out of town, then he drove home in the other direction. Thursday was not very far from Tuesday, and it was almost Wednesday now. He was suddenly starving, when sitting across from her he hadn't been hungry. He wished he'd taken the other half of the sandwich, but he had been too shy.

THURSDAY NIGHT, he was at the school before any-one else, and he waited in the truck, watching. One of the teachers showed up with a key, unlocked the side door, and turned on the light. When more people had arrived, Chet went to his seat in the back of the classroom. Beth Travis came in looking tired, took off her coat, and pulled a sheaf of paper from her briefcase. She was wearing a green sweater with a turtleneck collar, jeans, and black snow boots. She walked around with the handouts and nodded to him. She looked good in jeans. "KEY SUPREME COURT DECISIONS AFFECTING SCHOOL LAW," the handout said across the top.

The class started, and hands went up to ask questions. He sat in the back and watched, and tried to imagine his old teachers here, but he couldn't. A man not much older than Chet asked about salary increases, and Beth Travis said she wasn't a labor organizer, but he should talk to the union. The older women in the class laughed and teased the man about rabble-rousing. At nine o'clock the class left for beers, and he was alone again with Beth Travis.

"I have to lock up," she said.

He had assumed, for forty-eight hours, that he would go to dinner with her, but now he didn't know how to make that happen. He had never asked any girl anywhere. There had been girls in high school who had felt sorry for him, but he had been too shy or too proud to take advantage of it. He stood there for an awkward moment.

"Are you going to the café?" he finally asked.

"For about five minutes," she said.

In the café, she asked the waitress for the fastest thing on the menu. The waitress brought her a bowl of soup with bread, coffee to go, and the check.

When the waitress left, she said, "I don't even know your name."

"Chet Moran."

She nodded, as if that were the right answer. "Do you know anyone in town who could teach this class?"

"I don't know anyone at all."

"Can I ask what happened to your leg?"

He was surprised by the question, but he thought she could ask him just about anything. He told her the simplest version: the polio, the horses, the broken bones.

"And you still ride?"

He said that if he didn't ride, he'd end up in a wheel-chair or a loony bin or both.

She nodded, as if that were the right answer, too, and looked out the window at the dark street. "I was so afraid I'd finish law school and be selling shoes," she said. "I'm sorry to keep talking about it. All I can think about is that drive."

THAT WEEKEND was the longest one he'd had. He fed the cows and cleaned the tack for the team. He curried the horses until they gleamed and stamped, watching him, suspicious of what he intended.

Inside, he sat on the couch, flipped through the channels, and finally turned the TV off. He wondered how he might court a girl who was older, and a lawyer, a girl who lived clear across the state and couldn't think about anything but that distance. He felt a strange sensation in his chest, but it wasn't the restlessness he had felt before.

On Tuesday, he saddled one of the horses and rode it into town, leaving the truck. There was a chinook wind, and the night was warm, for January, and the sky clear. The plains spread out dark and flat in every direction, except where the lights glowed from town. He watched the stars as he rode.

At the school, he tethered the horse to the bike rack, out of sight of the side door and the lot where the teachers would park. He took the fat plastic bag of oats from his jacket pocket and held it open. The horse sniffed at it, then worked the oats out of the bag with his lips.

"That's all I got," he said, shoving the empty plastic bag back in his pocket.

The horse lifted its head to sniff at the strange town smells.

"Don't get yourself stolen," Chet said.

When half the teachers had arrived, he went in and took his seat. Everyone sat in the same seat as they had the week before. They talked about the chinook and whether it would melt the snow. Finally Beth Travis came in, with her puffy coat and her briefcase. He was even happier to see her than he had expected, and she was wearing jeans again, which was good. He'd been afraid she might wear the narrow wool skirt. She looked harassed and unhappy to be there. The teachers chattered on.

When the class was over and the teachers had cleared out, he asked, "Can I give you a ride to the café?"

"Oh—" she said, and she looked away.

"Not in the truck," he said quickly, and he wondered why a truck might seem more dangerous to a woman. He guessed because it was like a room. "Come outside," he said.

She waited in the parking lot while he untied the horse and mounted up. He rode it around from the bike rack— aware that he could seem like a fool, but elated with the feeling of sitting a horse as well as anyone did—to where Beth Travis stood hugging her briefcase.

"Oh, my God," she said.

"Don't think about it," he said. "Give me your briefcase. Now give me your hand. Left foot in the stirrup. Now swing the other leg over." She did it, awkwardly, and he pulled her up behind him. He held her briefcase against the pommel, and she held tightly to his jacket, her legs against his. He couldn't think of anything except how warm she was, pressed against the base of his spine. He rode the back way, through the dark streets, before cutting out toward the main drag and stopping short of it, behind the café. He helped her down, swung to the ground after her, gave her the briefcase, and tied the horse. She looked at him and laughed, and he realized he hadn't seen her laugh before. Her eyebrows went up and her eyes got wide, instead of crinkling up like most people's did. She looked amazed.

In the café, the waitress slid a burger and fries in front of Beth Travis and said, "The cook wants to know if that's your horse out back."

Chet said it was.

"Can he give it some water?"

He said he'd appreciate it.

"Truck break down?" the waitress asked.

He said no, his truck was all right, and the waitress went away.

Beth Travis turned the long end of the oval plate in his direction, and took up the burger. "Have some fries," she said. "How come you never eat anything?"

He wanted to say that he wasn't hungry when he was around her, but he feared the look on her face if he said it, the way she would shy away.

"Why were you afraid of selling shoes?" he asked.

"Have you ever sold shoes? It's hell."

"I mean, why were you afraid you couldn't get anything else?"

She looked at the burger as if the answer was in there. Her eyes were almost the same color as her hair, and ringed with pale lashes. He wondered if she thought of him as an Indian boy, with his mother's dark hair. "I don't know," she said. "Yes, I do know. Because my mother works in a school cafeteria, and my sister works in a hospital laundry, and selling shoes is the nicest job a girl from my family is supposed to get."

"What about your father?"

"I don't know him."

"That's a sad story."

"No, it's not," she said. "It's a happy story. I'm a lawyer, see, with a wonderful job driving to fucking Glendive every fifteen minutes until I lose my mind." She put down the burger and pressed the backs of her hands into her eyes. Her fingers were greasy and one had ketchup on it. She took her hands away from her face and looked at her watch. "It's ten o'clock," she said. "I won't get home before seven-thirty in the morning. There are deer on the road, and there's black ice outside of Three Forks along the river. If I make it past there, I get to take a shower and go to work at eight, and do all the crap no one else wants to do. Then learn more school law tomorrow night, then leave work the next day before lunch and drive back here with my eyes twitching. It's better than a hospital laundry, maybe, but it's not a whole fucking lot better."

"I'm from near Three Forks," he said.

"So you know the ice."

He nodded.

She dipped her napkin in her water glass and washed off her fingers, then finished her coffee. "It was nice of you, to bring the horse," she said. "Will you take me back to my car?"

Outside, he swung her up onto the horse again, and she put her arms around his waist. She seemed to fit to his body like a puzzle piece. He rode slowly back to the school parking lot, not wanting to let her go. Next to the yellow Datsun, he held her hand tight while she climbed down, and then he dismounted, too. She tugged her puffy coat where it had ridden up from sliding off the horse, and they stood looking at each other.

"Thank you," she said.

He nodded. He wanted to kiss her but couldn't see any

clear path to that happening. He wished he had practiced, with the high school girls or the friendly secretaries, just to be ready for this moment.

She started to say something, but in his nervousness he cut her off. "See you Thursday," he said.

She paused before nodding, and he took this for encouragement. He caught up her hand again and kissed it, because he had wanted to do that, and it was soft and cold. Then he leaned over and kissed her cheek, because he had wanted to do that, too. She didn't move, not an inch, and he was about to kiss her for real when she seemed to snap out of a trance, and stepped away from him. She took her hand back. "I have to go," she said, and she went around to the driver's side of the Datsun.

He held the horse while she drove out of the parking lot, and he kicked at the snow. The horse sidestepped away. He felt like jumping up and down, in excitement and anxiety and anguish. He had run her off. He shouldn't have kissed her. He should have kissed her more. He should have let her say what she wanted to say. He mounted up and rode home.

THURSDAY NIGHT he drove the truck in, no cowboy antics; he was on a serious mission. He was going to answer her questions honestly, such as the one about why he didn't eat. He was going to let her say the things she intended to say. He didn't wait for the crowd to arrive before going into the classroom; he went in early and took his seat in the back. The class filled up, and then a tall man in a gray suit with a bowling-ball gut came in and stood behind the teacher's desk.

"Miss Travis," he said, "found the drive from Missoula too arduous, so I will take over the class for the rest of the term. I practice law here in town. As some of you know, and the rest of you would find out soon enough, I'm recently divorced and have some time on my hands. That's why I'm here."

While the man talked on, Chet got up from his seat and made his way up the aisle to the door. Outside he stood breathing the cold air into his lungs. He let the lights of town swim in his eyes until he blinked them clear again and climbed into the rancher's truck. He gave it enough gas so the engine wouldn't quit, and it coughed and steadied itself and ran.

He knew Beth Travis lived in Missoula, six hundred miles west, over the mountains, but he didn't know where. He didn't know where she worked, or if she was listed in the phone book. He didn't know if it was he who had scared her off or the drive. He didn't know if the truck would make it all that way, or what the rancher would do when he found out he'd gone.

But he put the truck in gear and pulled out of town in the direction he had three times watched the yellow Datsun go. The road was flat and straight and seemed to roll underneath the truck, dark and silent, through a dark and silent expanse of snow-covered land. He stopped outside of Miles City, and again outside of Billings, to hobble around on his stiffened-up leg until he could drive again. Near Big Timber, the plains ended and the mountains began, black shapes rising up against the stars. He stopped in Bozeman for coffee and gas, and drove the white line on the empty road past Three Forks and Logan, to stay out of the ice that spread from the shoulder in black sheets. Somewhere off to his right in the dark, his parents were sleeping.

It was still dark when he reached Missoula, and he stopped at a gas station and looked up "Travis" in the phone book. There was a "Travis, B." with a phone number, but no address. He wrote down the number, but didn't call it. He asked the kid at the cash register where the law offices were in town, and the kid shrugged and said, "Maybe downtown."

"Where's that?"

The kid stared at him. "It's downtown," he said, and he pointed off to his left.

Downtown, Chet found himself in dawn light among shops and old brick buildings and one-way streets. He parked and got out to stretch his hip. The mountains were so close they made him feel claustrophobic. When he found a carved wooden sign saying "Attorneys at Law," he asked the secretary who came to open the office if she knew a lawyer named Beth Travis.

The secretary looked at his twisted leg, his boots, and his coat and shook her head.

In the next law office, the secretary was friendlier. She called the law school and asked where Beth Travis had gone to work, then cupped her hand over the receiver. "She took a teaching job in Glendive."

"She has another job, too. Here."

The secretary relayed this information on the phone, then wrote something down on a piece of paper and handed it to him.

"Down by the old railroad depot," she said, pointing toward the window with her pencil.

He pulled up at the address on the piece of paper at eight-thirty, just as Beth Travis's yellow Datsun pulled into the same parking lot. He got out of the truck, feeling jittery. She was rummaging in her briefcase and didn't see him right away. Then she looked up. She looked at the truck behind him, then back at him again.

"I drove over," he said.

"I thought I was in the wrong place," she said. She let the briefcase hang at her side. "What are you doing here?"

"I came to see you."

She nodded, slowly. He stood as straight as he could. She lived in another world from him. You could fly to Hawaii or France in less time than it took to do that drive. Her world had lawyers, downtowns, and mountains in it. His world had horses that woke hungry, and cows waiting in the snow, and it was going to be ten hours before he could get back to get them fed.

"I was sorry you stopped teaching the class," he said. "I looked forward to it, those nights."

"It wasn't because—" she said. "I meant to tell you on Tuesday. I'd already asked for a replacement, because of the drive. They found one yesterday."

"Okay," he said. "That drive is pretty bad."

"You see?"

A man in a dark suit got out of a silver car and looked over at them, sizing Chet up. Beth Travis waved and smiled. The man nodded, looked at Chet again, and went into the building; the door closed. Chet suddenly wished that she *had* quit teaching the class because of him, that he'd had any effect on her at all. He shifted his weight. She pushed her hair back and he thought he could step forward and touch her hand, touch the back of her neck where the hair grew darker. Instead he shoved his hands into his jeans pockets. She seemed to scan the parking lot before looking at him again.

"I don't mean any harm," he said.

"Okay."

"I have to go feed now," he said. "I just knew that if I didn't start driving, I wasn't going to see you again, and I didn't want that. That's all."

She nodded. He stood there waiting, thinking she might say something, meet him halfway. He wanted to hear her voice again. He wanted to touch her, any part of her, just her arms maybe, just her waist. She stood out of reach, waiting for him to go.

Finally he climbed up into the truck and started the engine. She was still watching him from the parking lot as he drove away, and he got on the freeway and left town. For the first half hour he gripped the steering wheel so hard his knuckles turned white, and glared at the road as the truck swallowed it up. Then he was too tired to be angry, and his eyes started to close and jerk open. He nearly drove off the road. In Butte he bought a cup of black coffee, and drank it standing next to the truck. He wished he hadn't seen her right away, in the parking lot. He wished he'd had a minute to prepare. He crushed the paper coffee cup and threw it away.

As he drove past Logan, he thought about stopping, but he didn't need to. He knew what his parents would say. His mother would worry about his health, driving all night, her sickly son, risking his life. "You don't even know this white girl," she'd say. His father would say, "Jesus, Chet, you left the horses without water all day?"

Back at the Hayden place, he fed and watered the horses, and they seemed all right. None of them had kicked through their stalls. He rigged them up in the harness, and loaded the sled with hay, and they dragged it out of the barn. He cut the orange twine on each bale with a knife and pitched the hay off the sled for the cows. The horses trudged uncomplainingly, and he thought about the skittery two-year-olds who'd kicked him everywhere there was to kick, when he was fourteen. The ache in his stomach felt like that. But he hadn't been treated unfairly by Beth Travis; he didn't know what he had expected. If she had asked him to stay, he would have had to leave anyway. It was the finality of the conversation, and the protective look the man in the dark suit had given her, that left him feeling sore and bruised.

In the barn, he talked to the horses, and kept close to their hind legs when he moved behind them. They were sensible horses, immune to surprise, but he had left them without water all day. He gave them each another coffee canful of grain, which slid yellow over itself into their buckets.

He walked back outside, into the dark, and looked out over the flat stretch of land beyond the fences. The moon was up, and the fields were shadowy blue, dotted with cows. His hip was stiff and sore. He had to pee, and he walked away from the barn and watched the small steaming crater form in the snow. He wondered if maybe he had planted a seed, with Beth Travis, by demonstrating his seriousness to her. She wouldn't come back—it was impossible to imagine her doing that drive again, for any reason. But she knew where he was. She was a lawyer. She could find him if she wanted.

But she wouldn't. That was the thing that made him ache. He buttoned his jeans and shifted his hip. He had wanted practice, with girls, and now he had gotten it, but he wished it had felt more like practice. It was getting colder, and he would have to go inside soon. He fished her phone number out of his pocket and studied it a while in the moonlight, until he knew it by heart, and wouldn't forget it. Then he did what he knew he should do, and rolled it into a ball, and threw it away.

RED FROM GREEN

T HE SUMMER SHE TURNED FIFTEEN, Sam Turner
took her last float trip down the river with her father.
It was July, and hot, and the water was low. Hardly anyone
was on the river but them. They had two inflatable Avon
rafts with oaring frames—Sam and her father in one, her
uncle Harry and a client from Harry's new law firm in the
other. In the fall, she would be a sophomore, which sounded
very old to her. She'd been offered a scholarship to a boarding school back east, but she hadn't officially accepted it
yet. Applying had been her father's idea, but now he looked

dismayed every time the subject came up. Everyone said what an opportunity it was, so much better than the local schools, but neither of them could bring themselves to talk about it.

Sam had been down the river every summer for as long as she could remember—in a dozen rainstorms, and in hot sun that burned the print of swimsuit straps into her shoulders. Harry, her father's younger brother, sometimes brought his friends, who passed the bottle of schnapps to her when her father was away from the campfire. She liked the smell better than the burning taste. She knew all the campsites and the cliff-shaded turns of the river, and the long flat stretch through pasture at the end. It was a four-day float trip, or five if you dawdled, or three if her father had to get back to work.

Her uncle's client was the reason they were on the river so late, when it was all sandbars and rocks. Sam hadn't been told that exactly, but it was the feeling she got—that they were going for this client. He had come from somewhere else, and was staying in Montana only for the case. She met him at the put-in, unloading the gear. Harry introduced her as his niece.

"You got a name?" the client asked.

"Sam," she said.

"Layton," the client said. He was younger than her uncle, and he wasn't tall, but he was big in the chest and arms. He set a full cooler on the ground and put out a hand to shake hers.

"God, I like being up here," he said. "I'm part Crow, part Blackfoot, part Sioux, I think. Part Jewish." His eyes were blue. He let her hand go. "You have perfect teeth," he said. "Did you have braces?"

"No," she said. She was awkward at fifteen, and praise made her suspicious.

Layton said, "This is gonna be fun."

Her father and Harry drove both empty trucks down-river to the place they'd take out three days later, to leave one and bring the other back. Sam stayed with the boats, and Layton volunteered to stay with her—to keep her safe, he said. They sat on the bank with the gear, sliding the coolers along the grass as the sun moved, to keep them in the shade. Sam was reading *The Thorn Birds*, bought at the supermarket along with the ice and groceries on the way out of town.

"It's not on your reading list," her father had said, dropping it in her lap in the truck. "But it's the best thing they had."

The boarding school had sent her a summer reading list with thirty books on it, books like *The Portrait of a Lady* and *Tender Is the Night*, but in her reluctance she'd forgotten to bring one along.

Layton took out a shotgun, to clean and oil it. "I bet

you're a crack shot," he said. "Montana girl like you. I bet you've got your own guns."

Sam shook her head and kept reading. He brought the gun over to show her the sight, which was just a notch of steel on the barrel. He crouched close to her shoulder and she could smell the oil on the gun.

"You don't need a fancy sight for a shotgun," he said. "You ever fire one?"

"No," she said. Her father had guns, but he hadn't been hunting since her mother died. Sam barely remembered her mother; she'd hit black ice driving to Coeur d'Alene when Sam was four. She sometimes wondered if her father had quit hunting because he'd been busy taking care of her, or if he'd just stopped liking to shoot things.

"Ho, boy," Layton said. He stood up. "We gotta take care of that. Get you a pheasant."

"It isn't bird season."

"No one'll know out here," he said. He ran a cloth over the barrel.

"There are houses on the river," she told him. "It's not very remote."

Layton laughed. "Re-mote. That's a good word."

She felt her cheeks heat up, but didn't say anything.

"I don't need *very* remote," he said. "Just a little remote."

Sam knew that her father wouldn't tolerate poaching, so she left it for him to take care of. But when he and Harry drove up, her father just looked hard at the shotgun and started loading his boat.

They put in that afternoon, and in spite of the low water they got to the first campsite before dark. Her father had a two-man tent for himself and a burrow for her—a waterproof sack just big enough for a sleeping bag, with a mosquito net at the top. She set up the burrow with her sleeping bag inside, and Layton and Harry built a fire and talked about the case.

Harry was childless, and had been jobless on and off. He had always seemed to take pride in being the wild younger brother—Sam's father was a district judge—but something had come over him a few years ago, and he had gone to law school and managed to pass the bar. He was a big man with a belly, and everyone liked him. He was trying to get out of debt, and the lawyer he had joined up with had given him Layton's case.

There were four other plaintiffs, all lab workers with neurological damage from exposure to organic solvents. One of them couldn't remember her children's names if someone nearby was wearing perfume. Diesel fumes, bathroom cleaners, scented soaps, new carpet—anything could set it off. Another had stopped driving, because she didn't always know whether a red light meant stop or go. Layton was a key plaintiff, because he had nothing in common with the women except the lab, where he had worked for a month on the wiring, and his tests matched all of theirs. It was good, too, to have a man involved; people were less likely to assume that he was inventing his symptoms. But his symptoms were milder, and he'd had to be cajoled into joining the lawsuit, and then into sticking around to go to depositions and have more tests. Sam guessed the river trip was part of the cajoling.

"I dunno," Layton said, standing over the fire ring. "I lose my car keys sometimes, but I did that before. I'm not very litigious. I might just take that job in Reno and scrap this whole thing."

Harry frowned at his tower of twigs. "When you could be here?" he said. "Fishing and hunting?"

"It's not even bird season yet," Layton said, and he winked at Sam. "If this thing drags out much longer, I'll go nuts."

Harry said nothing, but worked on the fire.

THE NEXT MORNING Layton was in the water before breakfast, fishing in waders, which no one ever brought in a boat on the river—they just waded out in shorts. He caught a little brown trout, clubbed its head, and threw it in the raft. Sam's father held the fish to the marks on the raft's rubber bow and said it wasn't big enough.

"Pull on the tail a little," Layton said. "It'll stretch." He was already moving back into the current, and the fish was dying. Sam saw Harry give her father a look, and her father put the fish in the cooler.

They packed up early and got on the river. Sam rode in the front of her father's raft, lying across the cooler that slid into the metal frame. She read for a while and then fell asleep with the sun on her back, waking to jump in the water and drag the raft over sandbars.

At camp that afternoon her father went fishing and she walked away from the river, up toward the hills. The grass in the open was pale yellow, and the path through the trees spiked with sunshine, but she was thinking about boarding school. She had a sense that she wasn't equipped for it. And she was wondering if she really had perfect teeth, and if anyone but adults would ever care. When Layton came through the trees she knew she'd wanted him to show up, though she hadn't known it before. His attention was different from other adult attention.

"I brought you something," he said.

She waited, but he kept on up the trail, and she followed him. They got over the first hill from camp, and up a second, higher one, and down again into a clearing. There weren't any farms or houses, and they were a long way from the river. Layton reached under his shirt and pulled out a small pistol, dark gray, with a short, square barrel. There was a fallen tree ten yards away, with small branches sticking up, and he stood an empty beer bottle upside down on one of the branches. The last of the beer stained the bark of the tree. Then he walked back and gave her the pistol. It was still warm from his skin, and heavy.

"Nine-millimeter Ruger semiautomatic," he said. "My pride and joy."

"Can they hear it?"

"I don't think so, with those hills," he said. "Anyway, we're legal. We're not killing anything."

He took her right hand and shaped it around the gun.

"One hand like this, arm straight, just like the movies," he said. He reached around her shoulders and positioned her left hand. "The other underneath." He kicked the instep of her right foot. "Bring this leg back."

Sam stepped back and pointed the gun at the bottle, not really breathing, with his chest against her back.

"Close one eye," he said. "Cover your target with the barrel. The gun's going to kick up, but it'll drop right back where you need it. You only need to squeeze a little." He let her go and stepped away.

She missed the bottle completely on the first shot, and the kick surprised her: the gun's explosion shot through her hands and shoulders and down into her legs. The second time she blew away the upended bottom. The third time she hit the broken-off neck. Then there was just a little triangle of glass sticking up from the tree.

"Go for it," Layton said.

She did, and hit it, and there was nothing left but a stub of branch.

"Hit the branch," Layton said.

And she did. She'd never been so proud of anything. Layton reached out and rubbed the top of her head, quick.

"She's a sharpshooter," he said. "You're not afraid of the kick yet, so you're not anticipating anything. You've got to keep that."

"Okay," she said. She could feel herself grinning like an idiot.

"Those perfect teeth," Layton said.

She closed her mouth and looked at the scarred tree where the bottle had been, which made her want to smile again, but she didn't.

"I'm sorry," Layton said.

"That's okay," she said.

When they walked back to camp, Layton veered off, so they came from different angles. Her father and Harry didn't say anything. Sam thought they must have heard the shots, but she figured it could have been Layton shooting alone. She had hit quarters propped in the tree bark, and made a smiley-face in a piece of paper. In the pocket of her shorts she carried an exploded hollow-point, which Layton said wasn't legal to buy anymore, and a warped quarter. Layton slipped the folded smiley-face into the camp garbage bag, and told Harry he didn't think there were pheasants out here at all.

Sam's father was making enchiladas, and chipping ice for margaritas with a pick. He made one without tequila for Sam. Layton asked for a virgin, too—alcohol made him nauseated since the work in the lab—and got out a little stereo with batteries. Sam's father said it would ruin the silence of nature, but pretty soon he was dancing at the cookstove, singing along with reggae covers. It was still light, and the swallows dived in the canyon. Her father two-stepped over with a big plastic spoon and a chip full of salsa, singing in falsetto, "No you ain't—seen—nothin' like the Might-y Quinn." He gave her the chip and kissed her on the forehead.

Her uncle Harry had too many margaritas and started talking about the case, about those poor, sick women with their lives ruined, and the gall of the lawyers who said they were making it up. When it got dark he went to bed. The other three sat close around the orange coals of the fire, and her father made up blues songs on the harmonica.

After a while, Layton said, "I need someone to walk on my back if I'm gonna row tomorrow. I'd ask you," he said to Sam's father, "but I'm guessing you weigh about two-fifty."

Her father didn't say anything, he kept playing harmonica.

Layton looked to Sam, who looked at the fire.

"It just takes a minute," he said. "I threw it out on a job, and rowing that boat messed it up."

Her father kept his eyes closed, the harmonica wailing. Sam stood up.

"Shoes off," Layton said.

She slipped off her sandals and left them by the fire. Layton lay on his stomach on the ground. "Okay, step on careful," he said. "Right in the middle." She stepped, squeezing the air out of his voice. "Now the other foot," he said. "Keep your balance." She could feel his ribs beneath her toes. "Now walk forward, slowly, then back," he said.

She did, and her father got up from the fire. "I'm beat," he said. "We should get an early start tomorrow."

Sam looked at him and he nodded, as if agreeing with himself. He put away his harmonica and disappeared into the dark where his tent was pitched. She could hear the rustle of nylon and the whine of the zipper, and then the night was quiet.

"One more time," Layton said. "That's so great. Now if you kneel with your knees between my shoulder blades, that's all I need."

She knelt like he said, lowering her hips to her heels, looking down at her bare knees and the short hair at the back of his head. "Now hold it there," he whispered. "Oh, God."

Then he didn't say anything. The right side of her body was warm from the fire, the left side was cold. It was too cold at night to be wearing shorts. She heard her father roll over in his sleeping bag inside the tent, nylon against nylon.

Layton's hand came back, and touched her hip. "You're tilted to this side," he said. She straightened. "There," he said, but his hand stayed on her hip. She thought about what to do. His eyes were closed and he seemed to have forgotten the hand. After a minute it slipped under the back of her thigh, touching her skin. She took his wrist and moved it away. The hand paused in the air, then slipped back under her thigh, over her shorts, touching between her legs with a shock like the jolt of the gun firing in her hands. She started to stand up, awkwardly, but he found her calf and pulled her back down. "Stay," he whispered.

She was on one knee, half-straddling his back in the dust, and he rolled over, facing her. His hand slid up her leg to the small of her back and held tight. His eyes were cloudy and intent, focused and unfocused, and she'd never seen a man look that way before.

She pulled away then, and he let her go, and she left the fire and climbed, trembling, into her burrow. She lay awake long after the moon rose, listening to the sounds in the camp: to her father snoring, and Layton finally putting out the fire, and the unzipping of his tent, and the rustle of his going to bed. She kept her hands between her thighs for warmth and the feeling there was sharp and aching, but she didn't know what to do about it except lie awake, breathing, until it went away.

WHEN SHE WOKE UP, Layton was out in the river again, walking downstream and casting at the banks. It was the brightest day yet, and a mayfly hatch hovered over the water, the current dimpled with the open mouths of rising trout. Her father poured the last of the hot water into the oatmeal in her cup, and she ate standing. In her shadow on the ground, she could see her hair, three days uncombed, sticking out on one side. She smoothed it down with her hand.

On the long flat stretch to the takeout, Sam rowed for a while. Her father pointed out a kingfisher in the brush along the banks, an osprey nest perched on the top of a tall tree. When she got the boat stuck on a rock, her father didn't say anything, but took the oars backward and pried it off. Layton and Harry stayed well ahead. It got hot, and she slipped off the raft and dropped under, feeling the cold current in her hair and clothes.

Layton didn't look at her at the takeout. They deflated the rafts and packed up the truck with the drained-energy feeling of a trip being over, and she changed into dry shorts in the trees. Her father drove and Harry had the other window, so she was squished with Layton in the middle, his left leg pressed against her right.

They dropped her uncle and Layton at the put-in with Harry's truck, and drove home in silence. Sam tried to keep her eyes open, but fell asleep. At the house, they unpacked the truck and hosed out the coolers, and when she gathered up her book and her river shorts, the hollow-point fell out of the pocket onto the grass.

Her father picked up the bullet, rolled it in his hand,

held it between his fingers. It was copper-cased, splayed out in a blossom of dull lead where the tip had been.

"Where'd you find this?" he asked.

"I shot it." She waited for the next question.

He said nothing, but held out the slug to her, and she took it.

He picked up one of the dry-boxes and carried it into the shed. For a while she listened to him unpacking, putting pots where they belonged, not noisily or angrily, just putting them away. Then she went into the house and filled out the final form for the scholarship to boarding school, and in the morning she put it in the mail.

She said nothing at first, and life went on as usual: she finished *The Thorn Birds* and saw her friends and ate dinners with her father. They talked about the weather and the cases he'd heard, and then after a week she told him that she'd accepted the scholarship.

He frowned at the table. "Oh," he said. "Good. That's great."

She wanted to ask why he had left her by the campfire, but instead she said, "Orientation is the last week of August. I should get a ticket."

"Sure," he said. "Right." He looked straight at her, and his eyebrows knit together. "I'll miss you here."

She felt a flood of warmth for him, an overwhelming feeling that it was a mistake to go away. He hadn't meant to leave her there. He hadn't known what would happen. He definitely hadn't meant for it to happen. Again she wanted to ask, to make sure, but instead she took her dishes to the sink, and the moment was over.

A FEW DAYS BEFORE she went away, there was a legal brief on the kitchen counter, with the names of her uncle's other plaintiffs but without Layton's. When she asked about it, her father said Layton had left for a job in Reno, and had taken himself off the case. He'd decided his symptoms weren't so bad and it wasn't worth it. He got little rashes under his eyes and he couldn't drink—so what? He'd needed to stop drinking anyway, he said. There wasn't anything keeping him in Montana, and it was too much of a hassle to stay involved from Reno.

Her father drove her to the airport, and carried her bag right up to the gate before saying, for the first time, that he didn't really want her to go. She cried all the way down the jetway, and the man in the seat beside her gave her a packet of Kleenex to stop her nose from running, and patted her shoulder when they landed in Salt Lake.

Someone from the airline told her where to change planes, and from Boston she took the bus she'd been told to take, though it seemed impossible that it could be the right one. She was red-eyed and nervous, but had decided that she didn't know anything, and the idea of going away was to learn.

Her dorm was in a cluster of stately brick buildings surrounded by trees, set apart from the little town, and the walls of her room had been painted over and over, for generations. She read *The Portrait of a Lady* there, and also *The Beach House* and *Candy*. Fifteen was old at boarding school. Most of the kids' parents didn't want them at home, and, knowing that, the kids seemed to know everything. A girl down the hall had done Ecstasy with her boyfriend back in Maryland, and had sex for three hours straight. Sam's roommate, Gabriela—whose last roommate got the Latin teacher fired—was surprised and impressed that Sam was a virgin.

There was a phone in the hall, and when Sam's friends from home asked for her, Gabriela said, "They sound so *western*." One of them, Kelley Timmens, had just sent Sam a letter about a boy they knew: *"We didn't have sex,"* she wrote, *"but imagine as <u>sick</u> as you can imagine—without having sex."*

Gabriela had laughed, reading the letter, and asked, "What does she mean?" Sam called home every week or two, and her father reported on people who'd asked about her, and she told him what she was doing in school. When she told him she was going to New York with Gabriela for Thanksgiving, he sounded startled. He said, "I'd get you a ticket home," though they hadn't talked about it before.

"I know," she said. "But it's two days of flying, for two days there." That had been Gabriela's argument.

"Where will you stay?"

"With her mom."

There was a silence on the line, and she imagined the quiet empty house around him.

"What happened to Harry's chemical case?" she asked.

"It got dismissed," her father said. "They needed that guy. What was his name? On the river."

"Layton," she said.

"Layton," he said. "You can't blame him. He wasn't really that sick."

"And the other people?"

"They can't work," her father said. "They have these awful headaches, all the time, and they can't go out."

"I'm sorry."

"It was a tough case," he said.

He asked a few questions about school, and then they said goodbye and Sam hung up, thinking about the woman who couldn't drive because the chemicals in everything made her forget which light meant stop and which go. She lay back on her bed under Gabriela's Charlie Parker poster and stretched her leg up to her face so her nose touched her knee, which was something Gabriela did. She brought the leg down and stretched the other one up.

She thought about the parties there were supposed to be in New York, and the boy from Exeter Gabriela was thinking about sleeping with, and the dime bag Gabriela was trying to get. She thought about her father eating dinner alone on the dark winter nights, with no one to talk to. And her friends—Kelley Timmens and the others—laughing in the hallway of her old high school, with its rows of lockers and the fluorescent lights reflected in the shiny floors. She thought about the pink cleaning stuff the janitors used, the smell of it in the mornings when she got to school, and the shampoo dispensers on the walls of the girls' gym showers that said "Montana Broom and Brush." She thought about her father nodding to her, after saying goodnight by the campfire, and about the aching feeling later as she lay in her sleeping bag, and how she hadn't understood what it meant. She smelled Gabriela's honey soap on the back of her wrist, and then her roommate walked in.

"Where *are* you?" Gabriela asked. "You're doing that spacey thing again."

Sam smiled. "No, I'm here."

"You're *not*. You're off in Montana or something. Do you have any letters from sick Kelley?"

"No."

Gabriela looked disappointed, but then she brightened. "I have to tell you what just happened in the library," she said. "You know that reading room you can lock?"

Sam nodded and rolled over to listen, tucking her pillow under her arms and her chin. The detergent on the pillowcase was Mountain Fresh. Gabriela flopped down on the new rug, and tossed back her long, conditioned hair. The rug was cream colored and Gabriela ran her hand across it, smoothing the fibers down. She looked a little flushed. "Okay, here's how it started," she said, and the story, full of longing and intrigue, began.

LOVELY RITA

IN 1975, Steven Kelly was twenty-three and newly or-
phaned. His father had died of pancreatic cancer two
years earlier, and Steven had quit a construction job to
move home and take care of his mother. She had relied on
her husband so absolutely, all her adult life, that she had
never filled a gas tank on her own, or looked at a tax form.
In her grief, after his death, she shifted her dependence to
Steven. She told him it was lucky she'd had a son, as if no
daughter of hers would be able to master a gas pump, either.
When she died of the same cancer as his father—one of the

doctors described it as mercifully quick, but there was nothing merciful about it—Steven felt like a boxer losing a fight, not knocked out but dizzy from the blows.

His mother showed him pictures when she was sure she was dying, of herself as a grave little girl in a white First Communion dress, with hollow-eyed Italian relatives in suits. She told him stories: her father had tried to start an ice cream business as a young man, but the unsold, unrefrigerated ice cream would melt by the end of the day, and he would end up eating it himself, dejected. Her mother had once won a beauty contest, scandalizing the family, in a bathing costume that came down to her knees. It was as if his mother was trying to make a safe place for her family in his brain. She died as she was becoming a real person to Steven, not just the more helpless of his ever-present parents, and so she was frozen in mid-transformation, neither one thing nor the other.

They left him the house he'd grown up in, but no money, once the taxes were paid. Their small Connecticut town, where he had spent a happy, bike-riding, bait-fishing childhood, was being transformed by the building of a nuclear power plant. When finished, the plant would pull in water to cool the reactors, which would raise the temperature of the river and kill all the fish he had grown up fishing. There were angry, impotent protests, and there were jobs for anyone who could wield a hammer. Steven hated the plant—everyone did—but he couldn't sell his childhood house, so he took one of the jobs.

The plant was two miles long and a mile wide, and still being laid with pipes. Steven was hired to build scaffolding for the pipefitters, then take it down and build it somewhere else. It was a union job, and they'd been told to make it last, so they worked in threes: while one worked below, the other two would climb to the top of the scaffolding and sleep. Someone usually duct-taped a transistor radio to the mouthpiece of one of the paging telephones, so music blasted through the plant. When the security guards got close to finding the radio, it would be rescued, and the music would stop, until the guards went back to their usual stations. Then the radio would move to another phone and the music would start again: "Born to Run" blaring over the clanging and drilling and sawing and hammering.

Steven's best friend from high school, Acey Rawlings, also worked at the plant. Acey had joined the Coast Guard for a while, but lost interest, and was home living with his mother. Any social status Steven had in school came from Acey's reflected cool, and now Acey had mythologized their teenage years, believing them to be as perfect as high school years could be. They had missed the Vietnam draft by the skin of their teeth, and Acey considered luck to be something they had rights to, and could count on.

Most nights after work, they went to the bar, to drink

beer until the hammering in their heads subsided enough for sleep. So in some ways nothing had changed since Steven was sixteen: he was still drinking beer with Acey, except now it was legal, and less exciting. It was on one of those nights that a girl showed up, hanging around. She was too skinny, with small tits and narrow hips, and she leaned on the bar next to Steven in jeans and a tank top and ordered a gin and tonic. He reflected that it was difficult not to talk to a girl standing next to you in a tank top, no matter how tired you were.

"Are you old enough to drink that?" he asked her.

She showed him her license. It said she was twenty-three, five-foot-six, 110 pounds. He could have lifted her right into his lap. Eyes: green; hair: brown. Her eyes were oversized, and ringed with green eyeliner and black mascara. He showed the license to Acey at the next barstool, because he could already feel that Acey's interest in the girl trumped his. He was going to have to get out of the way. Then he noticed the name on the card: Rita Hillier.

"I know you," Steven said.

"You do?"

"We went to grade school together. You moved away."

She narrowed her made-up eyes at him. "Did you have a lot of cavities?" she asked.

"No. I mean, not more than normal," he said.

"Did I ever kiss you?"

"No."

She shook her head. "Then I don't remember."

He could have told her that her father was the first person he had ever seen falling down drunk, but that seemed unfriendly. "You sat in front of me in Mrs. Wilson's class," he said. "You showed me how to cheat on spelling tests by keeping the practice list inside your desk, and pretending to look for an eraser."

"I did not."

"You think I don't know who corrupted me?"

"I remember cheating on math, later," she said. "Not spelling."

"Your dad used to walk you home from school."

Her eyes lost their gleam, and she looked at her drink. "That was me," she said. "They took his driver's license away."

"Is he all right?"

"I think so."

"Do you see him much?"

She frowned sideways at him. "You ask a lot of questions."

Acey kicked him under the bar.

"This is my friend Acey," Steven said. "We went to high school together, but not grade school. He doesn't ask so many questions."

Acey smiled his handsome smile at her, leaning forward over his beer.

Steven withdrew to the men's room to let Acey move

in. Behind the closed door, he stood looking at the filthy urinal, feeling disoriented by his brief return to third grade. Mrs. Wilson had caught him cheating on the spelling test, but he hadn't turned Rita in. It was his first and maybe only major act of chivalry. He got a zero on the test, and a C in spelling, but his parents had never asked about the sudden drop in his grade. He guessed that Mrs. Wilson had told them about the cheating and they were too embarrassed to mention it. Rita's dad wouldn't have cared if she cheated—the old drunk might even have applauded it, as wily—but it had seemed important to protect her from the disgrace.

When he went back out to the bar, Rita had her head bent close to Acey's, the deal sealed, and Steven put his arms around their shoulders.

"Let's go out for a midnight nuclear protest," Steven said, and Acey whooped with eagerness.

They drove down to the marina, stole a Sunfish from a slip, and sailed it across the river. Acey manned the tiller and Rita stood precariously in the bow and danced in the wind. When they got to the new plant, they yelled until the lights came on and the security guards came running down to the water to see what was going on. It was a pointless thing, hassling the security guards who were just local guys like them, getting a paycheck. But it felt good to yell on a warm night. Rita was surprisingly loud.

When the guards threatened them, fat and breathless in their tight uniforms, there wasn't any wind left to sail the Sunfish, so they laughed and paddled back for the marina with their hands. They could see a few stars through the haze. When they got back to the slip, Steven was starting to sober up. Acey left them to go pee off the end of the dock, and Rita said, "I'm sorry I got mad when you asked if I see my dad."

"That's okay," Steven said.

"I don't see him at all," she said. "I don't know where he is."

"I'm sorry."

"Do you remember him?"

"A little."

"What do you remember?"

"Not that much, really," he said. "I just remember him picking you up at school. He seemed like a nice man."

She looked at him skeptically, and he pretended he was telling the truth. Then Acey came back, buttoning his jeans. He bear-hugged Rita, kissed her hair, and took her home.

AFTER THAT, Acey was in love, and he couldn't shut up about it. He talked about Rita all the time, how amazing she was, how unlike other girls. He did it at the plant, where people weren't used to such happiness, and he made himself unwelcome. The married men only smiled and made jaded little jokes—*Wait until the blowjobs run out*—but the lonely ones found it intolerable. A raffle was held for a car someone needed to unload, with two packs of playing cards cut in half on the bandsaw, and Acey made a big show of buying a lot of tickets, and asking specifically for the heart face cards, so he could give the car and the winning card to Rita. There was open glee in the plant when he didn't win.

Even though Steven knew Acey was driving everyone nuts, and guessed there would be some attempt to take the Romeo down a notch, it still took him a minute to realize what was happening when a high, spooky voice came over the PA system one afternoon, filling the whole plant, calling, "Riii-ta, lovely Riii-ta!" Then it made a kissing noise and hung up.

The guys around them were already laughing, and Steven saw knowledge dawning on Acey's face. He thought he should have taken Acey aside long before and told him to keep his mouth shut.

The high voice came again, asking, "Rita, where *are* you?" Then the kissing noise.

Acey stalked to the closest paging phone, holding a wrench like a weapon, the guys still laughing behind him. No one was at the phone, of course. When Acey turned back with the wrench, he nearly bumped into a white hat, a liaison for the client. Normally someone saw the white hats coming soon enough for all the sleepers to get down off the scaffolding, but this one had appeared out of nowhere.

"Who's doing that voice?" the inspector asked Acey.

"I don't know," he said.

"Who's Rita?" the white hat asked.

Acey didn't say anything. The guys didn't, either.

"Tell me," the white hat said.

"It'll stop," Acey said.

"It better," the man said.

It did stop, until the next inspection. As soon as the white hat got there, the voice came over the loudspeaker again. "Riii-ta, darling *Riii*-ta!" And then the kissing noise. But by then it wasn't really about Acey or Rita. It had turned into a way of baiting the inspector, who went to their foreman, Frank Mantini, to complain. Someone who was standing outside the office heard Mantini tell the inspector it was a harmless prank, the guys letting off steam.

The white hat put a hundred-dollar bill on the fore-man's desk, according to the eavesdropper, and said, "It's yours if you find out who's doing this."

"I don't want the money," Frank said.

"Find out anyway," the white hat said.

Frank Mantini had a family at home, three daughters, and must have felt his job was at stake. But he couldn't stop the prank. If he caught one guy—which he couldn't—there would always be another to carry on. They switched tactics and started to torment him specifically. The high, spooky voice would say, "*Frank*-ie, you can't *catch* me!" and then make the kissing noise and hang up.

It went on for days, third-grade stuff: the occasional "Lovely Rita," sometimes a line of the Beatles song, badly sung, but mostly taunts for Frank. The white hat came in every day. Frank Mantini started to look ill, and people were saying that whoever was doing the phone stuff should lay off.

At the end of the week, Frank took Acey to the bar for lunch, to pump him for information. Some of the guys at the plant went to the bar at noon every day, and the bartender had their drinks lined up. They were career drinkers, old hands, and they drove back to the plant unimpaired. Frank Mantini and Acey weren't those guys. Acey came back drunk and decided to take a nap, not up on the scaffolding, but in a quiet corner on the floor. Frank had already gone into his office and shut the door.

Acey's quiet corner, where he had put his jacket under his head, was behind a parked front-loader, and someone went to use it. The poor guy climbed in, started the engine, and backed up, feeling a bump. He stopped and climbed down again to check what it was, and saw that he'd backed over Acey with one of the front-loader's heavy back tires, crushing his skull.

Someone tripped the alarm, and the ambulance came, pointlessly, and the white hat showed up. Frank Mantini got dragged out of his office, smelling of whiskey, and fell to his knees at the sight of Acey dead on the floor.

THE DEATH—the real weight of it—didn't hit Steven for a long time. He felt as if he was watching everything from behind glass. He got his old rod out and went fishing, and wondered why he and Acey had stopped going, why they stole boats to protest the plant but didn't take advantage of the last years of cold water and healthy fish. He didn't catch anything, and thought maybe the fish knew what was coming and had already cleared out.

The funeral was at St. Mary's, where his parents' funerals had been, and Steven sat in a pew like someone's accountant, thinking about what the flowers cost, and the casket. Frank Mantini, who had lost his job, was there without his family. Acey's little brother, the snotty kid they used to put in a head-lock, now a stocky nineteen-year-old with a crewcut, read from notes, his voice shaking, about how he would never have a big brother again. Acey's mother, who used to cook Steven eggs and muss his hair, tried to speak but couldn't. Then a big motherly girl with caramel-colored skin, Acey's first cousin, got up and helped everyone out by saying nice things without breaking down. Rita sat next to Steven, not crying. She had sobbed and screamed when he first told her.

After the funeral, Steven drove her home and they sat in his truck, talking about nothing, until finally she got out and went inside. He went back to his parents' house feeling like death was on him, a film on his face and grit in his teeth. He took a shower in his old bathroom, wishing he had a warmhearted girl like Acey's cousin to hold on to, and cried under the stream of water. In the morning, he got up to go back to the clanging plant.

R ITA CALLED HIM three days later and said, "I want you to help me hold a raffle."

"A raffle for what?"

"For me," she said. "I want to charge five dollars a ticket."

"What's the prize?" he asked.

"Me," she said. "I *said* that. For a night."

He thought about it: her skinny body, the odd waifishness. "No one's ever charged five bucks a ticket," he said.

"No one's ever got a five-dollar hooker, either," she said.

"Some of them might have," he said. "Some of them get it for free."

"I've seen the way they look at me," she said. "I think I can get five a ticket. That's five hundred and forty bucks, with two decks. If I could get ten, it would be over a thousand, and I could get out of here. But I don't know if I could get ten."

"It's illegal."

"So is every fucking thing that goes on at that plant," she said. "Jesus. Will you help me or not?"

He imagined himself pushing raffle tickets for Acey's girlfriend's pussy, for the girl who'd shown him how to cheat at spelling in third grade. "No."

"You have to."

"I don't have to do anything. No one's going to buy a ticket."

"They will, too. Just get me the cards, and I'll sell them myself."

"Get your own damn cards. You can cut them with scissors."

"It's not the same," she said. "It has to look like what they're used to. I need you to help me."

Steven hung up the phone and sat looking around his mother's living room, at the curtains she had sewn, now long faded, and the flowered couch where she had sat, missing his father and dying. It seemed strange now, their long marriage, their total dependence on each other. His father couldn't cook a meal or shop for groceries any more than his mother could gas up a car.

In the morning, on his way to work, Steven bought two decks of cards, one blue and one red. All he was going to do was give Rita the cut cards and let her do what she wanted, but Kyle Jaker, a kid on Steven's crew, saw him at the bandsaw and asked what the raffle was for.

"Nothing."

"Come on," Jaker said.

"Acey's girlfriend wants them."

"For what?"

Steven paused too long before saying, "I don't know."

"Oh, man, is it for her?"

Steven wondered how Jaker had guessed that, and moved away. "I said I'd get her the cards, that's all."

Jaker was scrappy and vain and pale-skinned, with a wild cowlick in the back of his carefully combed hair. It gave him a roosterish look. He skipped along beside. "How much?" he asked.

"She wants ten." Steven thought Jaker would balk at the price, and they'd be done.

Jaker pulled a twenty-dollar bill out of his wallet. "I'll take two," he said.

Steven had never seen a twenty come out so easily at the plant, or in the bar. Maybe not in his life, ever. "I'm not selling them."

"You just sold two. Come on."

He held the bill out and Steven finally took it, and dealt him two halves from the blue deck.

"The jokers!" Jaker said, grinning. "Jaker's jokers. That's good luck."

Word couldn't have spread faster if Steven had announced the raffle on the paging phones—which had gone eerily silent since Acey's death—and by lunchtime he had sold all of the blue deck and started on the red. He had agreed to meet Rita at the bar, and she climbed into his truck. He put the wad of bills and the blue stubs on the seat between them, and she grabbed the cash.

"I knew it!" she said.

"I hate this."

"I knew they'd buy them."

"You could get hurt."

"I can take care of myself," she said. She lifted her hips to tuck the cash away in her tight jeans, where it bulged. Then she put the blue stubs in her jacket and zipped up the pocket, like a kid putting away her milk ticket.

"There are other ways to get money," he said.

"I've tried them."

"Have you seen those guys?"

"You know I have."

"Why not just turn normal tricks?"

She gave him a level stare. "Do you know how many blowjobs it would take to make this much money?" She held out her hand for the other tickets.

"I'll sell them," he said. "You shouldn't have to do it."

Half the remaining tickets sold to the lunch crowd in the bar. The other half sold by the end of his shift. Some guys pretended to be helping out Acey's girlfriend, but most of them had a hungry glint in their eyes. She was a celebrity—Lovely Rita, muse of the pager-phone, the dead guy's girl. Steven thought he was getting an ulcer.

She was waiting outside the plant when he finished his shift. He walked toward his truck and she followed. Inside the truck, he gave her the money.

"What do we do now?" she asked.

"There's no *we* here."

"What do I do? To run the raffle."

"You put the cards in a hard hat and draw one out, and the holder of the other half wins."

"Where does it happen?"

"In the plant."

"Can we do it at the bar?"

"What the fuck is this *we*?"

"Can I do it at the bar?"

"You can't do it alone."

She blew her bangs off her forehead, exasperated. "Make up your mind," she said.

"I'll do it at work tomorrow," he said. He pictured himself standing in front of the hungry crowd, and he was glad he hadn't bought any tickets. If he won, having set up the raffle, they'd tear him apart.

"Thank you," she said, and she gave him back all the stubs, checking her pocket for ones that she'd missed.

He drove her home in silence, and she kissed him on the cheek—an odd, dry, sisterly kiss. Then she clambered down out of the truck and ran through the dark to her apartment. He drove home to bed and lay wide awake, until he rolled on his back and imagined himself the raffle winner. He whacked off like a teenager to put himself to sleep.

When he got to work the next day, early for his shift, the place was crawling with white hats. They were everywhere: talking to the crews, poking around. He assumed it was because of the accident, and Acey, but Kyle Jaker told him that one of the foremen had been caught diverting stainless steel to replace the pipes in his house.

"That's all?" Steven asked. The place looked like a kicked-over anthill.

"When's the raffle?" Jaker asked.

"I can't do it with all these hats here."

Jaker scanned the busy plant. "I should've bought more tickets," he finally said. "You got any left?"

"No."

"You got your own?"

"I didn't buy any."

Jaker raised his eyebrows at him.

"I forgot to," Steven admitted.

"So when's the raffle?"

"I don't know," he said. "After the white hats clear out."

"Hey," Jaker said. "I was just asking."

The white hats didn't clear out, and everyone was jittery. There were too many men on the floor, and they got in each other's way, with no one sleeping on the scaffolding. Steven kept waiting for someone to clap him on the shoulder, charge him with pandering, and throw him in jail.

Word started going around that the drawing would be at the bar, and the rumor became a kind of groundswell, it had its own momentum. The guys had given him ten bucks, or twenty, and they wanted a raffle. By the end of his shift, he had sweated through his shirt, and he changed to a new one.

He'd never seen the bar so packed. Kyle Jaker produced a hard hat and offered to do the drawing, so Steven gave him the cards. Jaker stood on a barstool and grinned down at the men standing shoulder to shoulder in the bar, staring up at him. He held the hat over his head and drew out half a card, slowly, as if performing a blood ritual. Then he held the card so everyone could see it. "Red-backed three of clubs," he announced. "Fuck, that's not me."

Everyone in the room dug in his pocket or looked at the stub in his hand. Finally Frank Mantini came forward. He'd left the plant, and Steven hadn't sold him any tickets. He handed Jaker a stub, and Jaker held it up to match the card he'd drawn. A sigh of disappointment rose up from the crowd, and there was a round of applause for Frank. Acey's ruined foreman seemed to have some kind of right to the girl. Then the men poured out the door to go home to their families, or to bed. The built-up, waiting tension in the room was gone.

"Congrats, Frankie," Kyle Jaker said. He clapped him on the shoulder and moved off.

Frank Mantini turned to Steven, still holding the cut card.

"Where'd you get that?" Steven asked him.

"I had twelve of them," Frank said. "Someone called me. I came down and bought what I could off the guys. I've got daughters her age."

"Don't start," Steven said. "I didn't want to get involved."

Frank handed him the halved three of clubs. A vein stuck out of his temple. He seemed to have more white in his hair than he had two weeks ago, but Steven could have imagined that. "You were Acey's friend, right?" Frank asked.

Steven nodded.

Frank shook his head. He looked hollow-eyed. "When you see her," he said, "would you tell her to knock this shit off?"

Steven said he would.

He drove by Rita's apartment after leaving the bar. He was thinking that if he had bought a ticket and won, he would have wanted his prize. He'd been thinking of her the way everyone else had, of her small hands and her wide mouth, of her straddling him with her skinny legs. She was the girl in the Springsteen song, if anyone was. *Wrap your legs round these velvet rims, and strap your hands across my engines.* Now he could wake her up and tell her she was free—he could be the good-guy hero. Or, he realized as he sat in the dark in his truck, he could pass off Frank's three of clubs as his own. She wouldn't know until it was too late. Frank Mantini would shit bricks, but Frank had already made his noble gesture, and gotten his satisfaction from that.

Steven was about to drive away, undecided, when Rita came outside. She was wearing a white nightgown with a pink ribbon woven through the neck, left untied in the front. She was barefoot and she had been crying, and she got in the truck. He could see the outline of her small breasts inside the white cotton, and her face looked naked with no makeup. "He's gone," she said. "He's gone."

"Acey?" he asked.

"No, this guy," she said. "My father—I wanted to find my father, so I got this missing-persons guy, you know, who finds people. He said he could find my dad, for sure. So I paid him, I gave him the cash, and he was supposed to look for my dad, and then he just, I don't know, left. And took the money. I'm so *fucking* stupid."

"I'm sorry," Steven said.

"But you know what?" she said. "I'm almost glad. I think he would've found out my father's dead."

"Why do you think that?"

"Because he never *looked* for me," she said, wildly, gesturing to the world outside. "He never *found* me!" Then she seemed to realize that he had never looked for her when he was definitely alive, and she deflated, shrinking into herself. "I don't know," she said. "No one can drink like that forever."

"Maybe he could," he said. "He was a tough guy."

She wiped her nose. "Yeah," she said. "So who won the raffle?"

"Frank Mantini," he said. "Our foreman, the one who was fired." He fished the card out of his pocket and gave it to her. "He bought a bunch of tickets. He doesn't want anything. He said he has daughters your age, and he wanted me to tell you to knock this shit off."

She looked at him, wide-eyed and forlorn, then made a small, anguished noise and covered her face with her hands. Her shoulders in the white nightgown shook. She crawled across the seat into his lap, fitting herself sideways between his chest and the steering wheel. Then she tucked up her legs and buried her wet face in his shoulder. He put his arms around her too-thin shoulders, carefully. Her hair smelled unwashed, but not in the way of adults: she smelled like an unshowered child, like summers at the public pool when he was ten.

They stayed there so long, Rita alternately sobbing and sleeping, that his arms grew stiff and the sky started to lighten. Rita finally woke, cried out, and extracted herself. At no point had she tried to kiss him, but he didn't try to kiss her, either. It wasn't because she was Acey's girl. It was because she seemed to be drowning, and might drag him under.

She wiped her nose with her hand. "What do you remember about my dad, really?" she asked.

He didn't say anything.

"You can tell me," she said.

"I remember he came to school one time to get you, in the middle of the day. He just showed up in the classroom, and he was drunk, I guess. I didn't really know that then. He knocked over a kind of easel thing. He called Mrs. Wilson by her first name and said he was taking you out of school. She said he couldn't."

Rita stared at him. "God, I don't remember anything," she said. "It's like a big eraser came through that part of my brain. Did I go with him?"

"I don't think so."

"Why didn't you tell me when I met you at the bar?"

"Why on earth would I tell you that?"

"Is that why you didn't want me? Why you handed me off to Acey?"

"I didn't hand you off," he said. "Acey grabbed you and didn't let go. He was crazy about you. He talked about you all the time."

Her face crumpled. "Really?"

He didn't want her to start crying again. He had to get out of the truck and stretch his legs. "Are you hungry?" he asked. He started the engine. "Let's get something to eat." Still in her nightgown, at a glossy diner table, she sat eating eggs and pancakes as if she'd never seen food before.

"Slow down," he said. "You're going to hurt yourself."

She licked maple syrup off her thumb. "I think I'm going to go away," she said. "Maybe find my brother. Do you remember him?"

"No."

"He was older. When we were kids we used to take care of each other. I wanted to be a ballet dancer, and he used to tell me I could, and he would draw pictures of the costumes I would wear. I remember that."

"Did you take dance lessons?"

"No." She laughed. "That didn't seem to matter. Hey, can I maybe borrow some money?" she asked. "Just a little bit. I gave so much to the guy, the detective. I guess he probably wasn't a real detective, was he?"

"Do you mean borrow, or keep?"

She made a pained face. "I don't know," she said. "I want to get on my feet. I'd want to pay you back."

After breakfast, he drove with her to the bank and gave her four hundred dollars he had earned building scaffolding with Acey. And then Rita vanished. It was a family talent. Steven drove by her apartment, and there was a sign saying it was for rent.

He went out fishing a lot, after that. Sometimes he would go at night and borrow a Sunfish like they used to, because it was so easy. Other times he would sit on a dock before sunset with a line in the cool water, watching the light play on the surface. He caught fish, not as many as he remembered catching as a kid, but enough to prove they were still there, waiting for food to come by, unaware that the river was only theirs until the plant started up, and then their time was over.

He finally left the plant, months before it was ready to open, not long before his job would have run out anyway. He sold his parents' house and moved to Florida, because there were plenty of jobs building houses there, and because it felt like a place everyone had moved to. It didn't seem like a place anyone was from. There were girls in the bars there, too, and sometimes he talked to them. If they didn't seem too crazy, he sometimes took them home.

There was one who moved in with him, who was a few years older than he was. She had been a mermaid at a water park, and she looked like a mermaid, with wavy blond hair. She showed him some of her act once, in the pool at his apartment building, with the kids coming out on the balconies to watch her do backward somersaults. It was convincing even without her green tail, and in that moment he thought he might love her. But he kept comparing the way he felt about her to the way Acey had seemed to feel about Rita, and it was a hard standard. After a few months he broke it off, and felt better. He didn't want anything that felt like it had a history to it.

When they started to drain a swamp where birds and fish had lived, for a new housing development down the road from his apartment, Steven watched the protests and the preparations with interest. The bird people were furious, the developers unmovable, and Steven was filled with relief that the fight wasn't his. Nothing here was his: the streets weren't full of things he'd done with Acey, or places he'd ridden his bike in grade school, and nothing reminded him of his dead parents. Even the old people were older than his parents had been. He thought there should have been something sad about how little he was tied up with the place, but instead it felt like freedom. He was free because it wasn't his water here, and they weren't his fish.

SPY VS. SPY

ONE JANUARY EVENING, when the doctor's new house felt warm and inviolable against the wind and cold outside, his younger brother called. They hadn't spoken for months. Aaron assumed George wanted something: a larger share of what their parents had left them, or a loan, or some other favor that would annoy him. But George's desires were hard to predict, and what he wanted, this time, was to invite the family skiing, over Presidents' Day. A new girlfriend had put him up to it, he said. She thought they should spend time together. It bothered Jonna—that was the girlfriend's name—that the brothers spent Christmas apart.

She worked with George as a ski instructor, and she craved a family, not having had enough of one to understand what a pain in the ass it was.

"So are you inviting us skiing or calling me a pain in the ass?" Aaron asked.

"Don't be a jerk," his brother said.

"*I'm* the jerk?" Aaron wished he could play a recording of the phone calls for a third party and get some satisfaction, but George usually managed to make him sound childish, too.

"Just say no," George said. "So I can tell Jonna you don't want to."

"Tell her no yourself."

"I can't."

"Then get a new girlfriend."

"She *is* a new girlfriend. That's why I can't say no."

"Since when is Presidents' Day a family holiday?"

"Oh, hell, Aaron," George said. "It's a weekend people go skiing. She just thinks we should get together."

"Do we have to chop down a cherry tree? Recite the Gettysburg Address?"

"I'll tell her you said no."

"We're coming," Aaron said, before George could hang up. It was not the first time he had done something solely because his brother seemed to want him not to. He would have to ask his wife, and Bea would remind him of his altitude sickness and his constant fighting with George, but he could manage all of that. "We'll be there," he said.

"Suit yourself," George said, as if the trip were Aaron's idea. "Make sure you bring Claire."

"I'll see if she's free."

"I already asked her," George said. "She's in. You just have to fly her home."

Aaron hung up and spent the rest of the evening fuming at George's presumption. Aaron's daughter, Claire, was now a sophomore in college, but he didn't think of her as someone who could be invited separately on a trip. She was the little girl who had climbed on his head, who had asked him if people could see inside her mind, who had loved his old *Mad* magazines as he thought no girl had ever loved *Mad*, giggling at them while he read the paper, asking sometimes to have things explained. Into her teens she had stayed home on weekend nights and watched old movies with him, curled under his arm on the couch, while Bea wandered off, losing interest. He could still feel the weight of his daughter's head against his chest, and see, cast in silver light from the TV, the rapt absorption with which she watched. The only movie they disagreed on was *Rebecca*. It was his least favorite Hitchcock, but she loved the sweet, simple girl meeting the rich man with the dark secrets: "I'm asking you to marry me, you little fool," shouted from his hotel dressing room.

His brother might have despised Claire, since he hated everything else Aaron had. He liked to say that Aaron's career as an orthopedic surgeon was mercenary, his marriage to a fellow doctor bourgeois, and his modest house on a hillside an environmental nightmare. So he might, by extension, have declared Claire a spoiled, entitled brat. But Claire wasn't spoiled, and George loved his niece. He had courted her from the time she could walk and talk, bringing her presents from his adventures. He played invented games with her, endless games for which no one else had patience. In her favorite, he was the Fire, chasing her around the house and the backyard, never quite catching her, while she squealed with terror and glee. Aaron had tried to be the Fire a few times, out of fatherly duty, but he didn't do it with the correct enthusiasm. Claire tried to direct him but soon lost interest. She could play it for hours with her uncle.

When she was old enough, Claire learned to ski. She was fearless, and George advanced the theory that the fearlessness came somehow from him.

"How do you think that would work?" Aaron had asked.

"She didn't get it from you two," George said. "You're both so conservative."

"No we aren't."

"In terms of your life choices."

"Maybe we made her feel safe," Aaron said. "So she can be brave."

"It seems genetic," George said. "It could be. Diabetes is passed that way—over and down, like a knight in chess."

"No it isn't!"

"Yes, it is."

"There's no gene for bravery that you have and I don't," Aaron said.

"Then maybe I taught her to be fearless, by playing those games."

"Why don't you have your own kids and speculate about *their* character traits?"

"If I were having a kid," George said, "you'd just tell me I couldn't afford it."

And that was true.

Aaron didn't like George's courting of Claire, and didn't like George inviting her skiing before he invited Aaron and Bea, but he couldn't keep her from his own brother. She might need bone marrow someday, he told himself. She might need a kidney. Also there was the fact that Claire loved her uncle. So they went off to ski, for Presidents' Day, because George had ambivalently asked them to.

THE FIRST MORNING, they all met in the gondola line. Jonna, the new girlfriend, flashed a nervous, welcoming smile, and Claire, back from California on a ticket that wasn't cheap, hugged her tightly. Then she hugged George. Claire's cheeks were pink with health and cold and happiness, and she wore a blue fleece hat that said UCLA on it. She asked Jonna questions as the gondola rose, and Aaron was inordinately proud of her: she was so vibrantly young and engaging and unself-absorbed.

Jonna, on the other hand, was a puzzle. If Aaron had met her on the street, he wouldn't have pegged her for a ski instructor. She didn't seem hardy or sporty or gregarious; she seemed delicate, prickly, and undernourished. She was wiry, about thirty-five, with a peroxide-white cloud of hair around her face, and a small diamond stud in one nostril that must have been hell in the cold. Aaron gave silent thanks that Claire had not gone in for piercing her face. Then he heard Jonna say that her father was a lift operator when she was a kid, so she skied for free, tagging along after the instructors in place of being babysat. That made sense. She was a ski brat the way people were military brats, and it had made her insecure. That was typical of George's girls. He liked them needy and dependent, the opposite of Bea, who ran an emergency room and was born to command. The puzzle solved, Aaron stopped listening and watched people make their way—some quick and graceful, and some in a slow, shuddering slide—down the mountain below.

At the top, Claire went off with George and Jonna, the better skiers, and Aaron stayed with his wife. Bea never left the groomed runs where she could make long, easy turns all day without breaking a sweat. Years in the ER had left her with no attraction to danger. On the chairlift, they compared notes on Jonna. Bea guessed it wouldn't last, that Jonna wouldn't be able to buoy George up the way he needed.

"There's a look little girls have who are adored by their fathers," Bea said. "It's that facial expression of being totally impervious to the badness of the world. If they can keep that look into their twenties, they're pretty much okay, they've got a force field around them. I don't know if Jonna ever had it. I think she's always known about the bad things."

"Does Claire have the look?" Aaron asked.

Bea turned to look at him, with amused affection behind her goggles. "Are you kidding?" she asked. "With you and George both? She'll have it when she's eighty. She'll never get rid of it."

T HE FIVE ALL MET for lunch, piling hats and gloves on a long table, with the snow melting on their unbuckled boots, carrying cheeseburgers and fries on cafeteria trays. George was slowed by handshakes and questions from people he had taught to ski, and when he finally brought his tray, he squeezed between Claire and Jonna.

"Eight bucks for a veggie burger," he said. "It's like Aspen around here. Rich doctors like you, crowding the slopes and driving the prices up."

Aaron said nothing and started on his second beer. It

was so good and so cold. His brother was only joking, looking for attention, having gotten so much from the rest of the cafeteria. His ski students clearly loved him, and that seemed touching. Aaron's patients didn't love him that way. People loved their GPs and their dermatologists, but not their orthopedists. They saw him only under duress, and he gave them frustrating news. "George," he said. "We should ski together this afternoon."

"All right," George said warily, pounding the ketchup bottle over his yellowish soy patty.

"You act like I want to push you off a cliff."

"Maybe you do." George resorted to a knife, and the ketchup slid out along the blade.

"You should take me on the good stuff."

"You can't handle the good stuff."

"Sure I can."

"Honey, you don't always do well at eight thousand feet," Bea said. "And you've had two beers."

"See?" his brother said. "Listen to your wise wife."

Aaron didn't like to be reminded of his debility—no one else got sick at this altitude—and he was doing fine. "Did you take Claire on the good stuff?" he asked.

"Dad," Claire said.

"Claire's a really good skier," George said, through a mouth full of soy.

"I know she is. I taught her."

"*I* taught her," George said. "And she's thirty years younger than you are."

"But you're only five years younger."

"But I ski every day. Stop staring at my veggie burger. Eat your own goddamn burger. Your dead cow corpse burger."

At twenty, George had dropped out of college to go cycling around France with a girl, and he became a vegetarian under her influence. At the time, Aaron had defended George's decision to leave school to their parents. He had admired and envied his brother's bravery—he was already in medical school and wouldn't have known what to do without the structure of classes—and he thought it important that George be allowed to find his own way. Also, in his secret heart, he was glad his brother wouldn't be a doctor, too; the medical profession wasn't big enough for both of them. So he had told the parents to back off. But it seemed, so many years later, that it was time for George to drop the lingering no-meat affectation, or at least to stop proselytizing. "Look, you can eat soy protein if you want," he said, "but why harangue other people?"

"I'm just thinking of your arteries," George said.

"My arteries are fine. Who decides to stop eating meat in *France*? You could have come back from that trip looking tan and healthy and full of steak béarnaise, and instead your skin was *gray*."

"Boys," Bea said. "Please don't fight. For once."

"We're not fighting, we're talking," George said. "It's not just about health. There's a movie you should see, about slaughterhouses. Claire, you should see it. I'll give you the DVD."

"Please don't give my daughter an eating disorder," Aaron said.

"It's not a disorder!"

Jonna stood, digging her coat out of the pile. "I'm going skiing," she said, glaring at them both. She pulled her jacket onto one arm and rocked determinedly toward the door in her stiff-bottomed boots. She had a tattooed sun on the back of her neck, below the white-blond puff of hair, and it disappeared as she shrugged the coat up onto her shoulders.

Bea looked at George, as if expecting him to follow. "Aren't you going?"

He held up his ketchupy hands. "She wants to ski alone," he said.

Bea sighed, and dropped her paper napkin on her tray. "Claire, can you stand to ski the boring stuff with me?" she asked.

"Yes, please," Claire said. She draped an arm over her father's chest, planting a kiss on the top of his head. Aaron resisted looking at George in triumph, but then Claire whispered, *"Be good,"* into his hair, which lessened his sense that he'd won this round.

Bea and Claire weaved through the crowded, noisy cafeteria, and the brothers watched them go. Even bundled in ski clothes, the two women had a matching grace. *Women.* It was so strange to see Claire that way.

"Do you and Bea still fuck?" George asked.

"Just stop," Aaron said. "You've done enough for one lunchtime."

"How often?" he asked. "Like, once a week? Once a month? Once a *day*? Do you take pills?"

Aaron started to pull on his coat. "Knock it off."

"What about Claire, do you think she's a virgin?"

Aaron grabbed his gloves and stalked away, but he was slowed by the staggering gait of the boots, which made him feel ridiculous. He couldn't even storm out. He'd never been able to. He turned and asked, "Are you coming or not?"

THE TWO BROTHERS were on the highest chairlift, headed for the top of the mountain, and Aaron had calmed down. Life with George was like interval training—it was possible for Aaron to get his heart rate up and then quickly down again, from constant practice. He was admiring the trees gliding past, the white mare's tails against the blue sky, and he thought of the winter he and George, as boys, were on a makeshift ski team, coached by another boy's father, taking turns practicing slalom gates and taking jumps on their old wooden skis. George must have been about nine, and he was already the better athlete, instinctive and efficient, where Aaron was always thinking things through, using too much energy and movement, a gawky teen. He thought how spectacular it had been to watch George take the gates, and how proud he had been of his talented little brother. They were confederates, on that team of boys they didn't know well, as they couldn't normally be, when Aaron was in high school and George still learning to spell. They rode back home on the ski bus side by side, making jokes. He was about to ask George if he remembered the team, when his brother started in.

"How much money do you think you have?" George asked.

"You know, I was just enjoying this beautiful day," Aaron said.

"Is it close to a million? Just ballpark. Not counting real estate."

"George."

"*Getting and spending, we lay waste our powers.* I read that in college. It had a big effect on me. Do you think you're wasting your powers, getting money, when you could be out here all the time?"

"Why do you do this?"

"Do what?" George asked. "You never want to talk about anything real. You just cut me off. Like you must have a guess about whether Claire's fucking. I know you think about it."

Aaron imagined taking his brother's parka in his hands and swinging him forward off the chairlift. He was strong enough, and had surprise on his side. They hadn't brought down the safety bar over their legs. The only danger would be George pulling Aaron down with him. Aaron might break a leg, tear an ACL, become one of the miserable patients he saw every day, facing the loss of their mobility and their youth. He could be arrested, even. But at least it would all be over between them, no more attempts at family vacations, no faked brotherly love.

"She has a new boyfriend, you know," his brother said.

That was news to Aaron, and hearing it from George was like the stab of a pocketknife in his heart. Not a wound that would kill him, but quick and painful and precise. He pretended it wasn't news.

"You didn't know, did you?" George asked. "He's pre-med. He'll be a sawbones like you. You'd think she'd be proud to tell you."

"Why ask us here?" Aaron managed to say. "Why ask for a family ski trip and then do this?"

"I'm just trying to have a real conversation, like human beings," George said. "About real things. To be close, like a family for once, instead of just riding up the lift saying 'What a beautiful day' like a bunch of tourists from Minnesota."

"I've said nothing of the kind."

"She's an adult, you know? You treated her like an adult

when she was a little kid and you treat her like a little kid now that she's not."

Aaron was startled. "Is she complaining?"

"No—*I* am! You think you're always right about everything, but you're not. I know a few things, too, you know? You'd think I'd be allowed to ask you a fucking question now and then."

Aaron stared at his brother in amazement, but they were at the top of the hill, and had to lift their ski tips and shuffle forward on the icy ramp as the chair discharged them, a process that always felt infantilizing to Aaron, because he had learned it when he was a child, or because it was so awkward to lose momentum after the majesty of riding through the air. George seemed to experience no discomfort, but then he was used to it. It was his job.

They stood at the top of the lift, at the top of the mountain, with people poling past them. Aaron had a headache, and wished he'd never agreed to come skiing. Would he never learn? A small child in a helmet, ski tips together in a snowplow, dropped bravely off the edge. Claire had been that young when she started, her hair bunching out of a purple headband. She had been so brave and so small, and now she was sharing a bed with a callow premed who might not understand—who couldn't understand—how important it was to her father that she stay safe and protected and well.

"I tried to get Claire to smoke pot with me once, but she wouldn't," George said.

The air felt very thin in Aaron's lungs.

"Most kids would have taken the joint," George said. "I think she knew you wouldn't want her to. She's loyal to you."

"Is this your peace offering?"

"If you want to see it that way."

"Let's just ski."

"I bet she's smoked some by now."

"Take me on the good runs."

"That's a bad idea."

"You can bait me, or you can protect me," Aaron said. "But you can't do both. Where's the good snow?"

George shrugged, and they skated and sidestepped and skied to a place where the slope divided: an easy blue-square run on the left, and a black diamond posted on the right, with a rope strung between two poles, barring access.

"This is the best run here," George said.

"It's closed off."

"We'll go under the rope."

"I could lose my ski pass," Aaron said. "You could lose your job."

"It's not closed for avalanche. They're just roping it off to keep down the broken legs, because all the once-a-year bozos are out for the long weekend."

"Like me?"

George shrugged again.

"Let's stay on what's legal," Aaron said.

"I thought you wanted the good stuff."

"Not if it's off-limits."

"The best runs are always off-limits," George said. "Off-piste. *Interdit*."

"*Interdit?*" Aaron said. One bike trip at twenty, and George thought he was on the French cycling team.

"It's not a bad run," George said. "I promise. I take it all the time. Even you can do it."

Aaron looked to see if anyone was coming down the mountain behind. No one was, so he followed his brother, ducking under the orange rope that George held for him, feeling a little dizzy as he straightened. Then his head cleared and they were on the other side. The whole mountain was below them, the trees in sharp focus, ice crystals floating in the air. He felt a rush of exhilaration at having broken the rules. He had been such a good student, a dutiful doctor, a faithful husband. Maybe he should have flouted authority more in his life, been more like George, ducked the ropes, been the Fire. The slope didn't look that bad. A little steep.

George had already taken three neat turns straight down the steepest part. Aaron carved his way around the side; he didn't have George's control. A few times his edges skidded, and his legs felt shaky. The snow was deep but not always soft. Aaron's headache had returned, or he had begun to notice it again. He felt thirsty, in spite of the two beers. He regretted the beers.

They skied down to a second steep slope, George still well ahead, and Aaron stopped to catch his breath and rest his knees. Bending over to stretch, he had an attack of vertigo, followed by nausea. For a moment he blamed the burger, but then he recognized the feeling, and understood his growing headache. Bea had been right, that he had forgotten what altitude sickness was like, and how quickly it came on. She had brought a physician's sample of the pills, but he had told her he didn't need them, and was too old to be stressing out his kidneys. He sat dizzily against the hillside, to rest a minute.

He heard a shout, and squinted at the small figure of his brother below, against the white slope. The distant George patted his hand on his head to ask if everything was all right. They had learned the signal as kids in canoes. Aaron didn't think he could stand, but he patted his head anyway: *Everything's fine.* He tried to push himself to his feet, slid a few yards on the backs of his skis, and collapsed into the snow again. There was another shout from George, a more urgent hand signal, which Aaron didn't bother to answer.

If they'd had it out when they were younger, really whaled on each other, then maybe it would be out of their systems. They could be civilized to each other now. But George had always been younger, and Aaron too restrained to take advantage of his greater strength. By the time they were the same size, Aaron was in college and didn't think about his brother. And if he *had* thought about it, he'd have realized that George could already beat him. He lifted his head and patted the top of it, to show that he was on his way down, but George had started side-stepping up the mountain. He was coming at a good clip. The nausea surged again, and the remains of Aaron's burger came out in a soupy mess in the snow, between his knees. He coughed, with the taste of bile in his throat. George would never let him forget being rescued from his own puke on the closed black-diamond run. The story would be hauled out every time they were together: *Remember that time?* George would regale Claire with her father's weakness, and Claire would be caught between them, sneaking her father guilty looks.

He struggled to his feet and stood uneasily, resting on his poles. Then he dug his edges into the hillside and tried to ease into a turn, but lost his balance and fell to his downhill side. It all happened very quickly. The skis went into the air as he rolled, and rolled again. One ski released and skidded free, and the other wheeled with him, and then he slammed into something that turned out to be his brother. They tumbled, and came with George's help to a tangled stop.

Aaron groaned, and tried to sit up. He felt warm wetness near his eye, and took off his glove to feel a gash on his forehead that must have been from the edge of a ski, though how and whose, he wasn't sure.

"Why didn't you move?" he asked his brother.

"I didn't have time," George said. "You could have died, hitting a tree."

"I could have died hitting *you*."

"That's my fault?"

"I have to get to a lower elevation," Aaron said. "The altitude."

"Were you puking?"

"No."

"I saw you."

Aaron looked down the hill. He could see the lodge in the distance, the parking lot full of tiny cars. It was such a long way. "I have to get my ski," he said.

They tried to stand, and Aaron put his hand on his brother's shoulder for support. George snarled at him like a wounded dog, and pushed his hand away. "It hurts," he said.

Aaron reached to investigate the pain in George's shoulder—it was what he did all day—and George knocked his arm away with a hard blow, and then they were grappling, oddly, clumsily: one of them on two skis with one good arm, and the other on one ski with one glove, weak with nausea. But they were fighting, finally, and it was an odd relief. George shoved an open, gloved hand into Aaron's face, the cold leather squishing his nose. Aaron grabbed George's hair with his bare fingers. They teetered and swayed on the skis, scrabbling for purchase on each other's slippery coats, trying to stay upright and also shove at each other. George connected once with Aaron's ribs, without leverage, and they almost went over, then compensated as if they were dancing: slapstick fools. They slid sideways down the hill a few feet, plowing snow. George tried to push him away, but Aaron got an arm around his brother's legs, and they fell in a heap. George, protecting his shoulder, nearly crushed Aaron's windpipe with his elbow.

They lay panting and coughing in the snow. Aaron waited for the icy flush of adrenaline to fade, and remembered the time he had been assigned to keep an eye on George, who was still in diapers, in the front yard. Aaron was no more than seven, absorbed with the fort he was building, and his little brother had wandered off and fallen into a ditch with some water in the bottom of it. Aaron was sent to bed without dinner when a muddy George was recovered, and their father didn't speak to him for days. He regretted the punishment, but he had also been disappointed in a way he couldn't have articulated then, that the problem of his brother hadn't solved itself.

I N THE BIG comfortable new lodge—a hideous pimple on the nose of the mountain, according to George— there was a massive stone fireplace surrounded by couches and chairs. On the walls were heavily framed oil paintings of western scenes: cowboys and Indians on the Plains. Bea sat on the upholstered arm of one of the chairs, looking concerned and exasperated. She'd bought a can of recreational oxygen for Aaron in the lodge's gift shop: not an old man's green tank but a sporty blue cylinder, like a can of shaving cream. He was bruised and sprained and had three stitches in his forehead, but he felt beautifully high on the oxygen in the deep, soft couch, and his headache was gone. The young doctor who stitched him up told him he could have broken his neck in that fall. He could have died, or spent his life in a wheelchair, and he should stick to slopes he could ski. Aaron accepted the insult and the medical condescension with equanimity. He was intensely happy to be alive and whole. Beneath all his bruises there was the good, honest muscle soreness of skiing, and beneath his wife's consternation was love, and worry. He might even love his brother in a mood like this, and he looked at George with curiosity, to see if he did.

His brother lay sideways on the other couch, with his head in Jonna's lap and his feet on the cushions. He had cadged a Vicodin somewhere, which he couldn't possibly need for his shoulder. He had a torn labrum, probably, and it would need surgery, but it was easily fixable.

"I can't believe you took him outside the ropes," Bea said.

"He wanted to go!" George said. "You heard him begging me at lunch. You can't tell him no."

"He looks like he's been in a prizefight."

"I'll be all right tomorrow," Aaron said. "Back on the slopes."

"You'll be lucky if you can walk tomorrow," Bea said.

Claire came in with a tray of white porcelain cups. Her smooth face was freckled from the day in the sun, her hair freshly braided, and she had changed into jeans and a blue fleece pullover. She was the best thing Aaron had done. "I had them spike the coffee," she said.

"Sweet Claire," George said. "Heart of my heart."

"Whiskey, caffeine, and Vicodin?" Bea asked.

"It won't kill me," George said.

And it was true, nothing would. The knowledge broke over Aaron in a wave, through his oxygenated good mood. They were bound like two dogs with their tails tied together, unable to move without having some opposite effect on the other, unable to live a single restful minute without feeling the inevitable tug. George would be courting Claire from his nursing home, lobbing insults at Aaron from cover, inhabiting his dreams. Right now he was sipping his spiked coffee complacently, while Jonna stroked his hair.

"Tomorrow I'm going to be the Fire," George said to Claire. "And chase you around the lodge."

Claire rolled her eyes and smiled at her uncle, a smile that gave Aaron a twinge of jealousy. She took the tray back to the bar—responsible girl. Surely she was using birth control with the premed boy. Aaron didn't want to know what kind, just as he didn't want to think about the images

George had put into his head. He felt the hot coffee and whiskey make their way down to his stomach before the double warmth was more generally absorbed. Bea wasn't going to stroke Aaron's hair; she wasn't even going to sit next to him.

On the other couch, George had his eyes closed in Jonna's lap and his coffee cup on his chest. "We should do this next year," he said. "We should do this every year."

TWO-STEP

IT WAS SNOWING ALREADY, in late September: a freak-
ish, early snow that came after days of crisp and sunny
fall weather. The other resident physicians at the hospital,
the ones who had been in Montana two and three years, or
all their lives, told Naomi this was nothing. "Wait till it
snows in August," they said. It was a Sunday, and Naomi
had the day off, and she was sitting in the clean, bright
kitchen of her friend Alice's renovated Victorian, while Alice cried at the kitchen table. Alice was lanky and boyish
and had always seemed supremely resilient, but now she
was splotchy with tears and her nose was running.

"But how do you *know*?" Naomi asked.

"I just do," Alice said. She blew her nose in a tissue. "I can feel it. His mind is somewhere else."

"Maybe it's just work. We're all tired."

Alice shook her head. "It's not that," she said. "He loves the hospital. Do you want tea or something?"

She got up to put the kettle on, and Naomi didn't protest. The cupboards were painted white, and the open shelves held blue and green dishes. A window over the sink looked out on the snow. Naomi and her husband were renting, and neither of them had the time or the inclination for decorating—they still had cardboard moving boxes as end tables—but Alice had left some kind of design job behind in Los Angeles, and she clearly had skills.

"This kitchen is so pretty," Naomi said.

"I *know*," Alice said, and she made a little wailing noise. "I love this house. We were going to live here for the rest of our lives. I'm sorry to dump all this on you. It was nice of you to come."

"But maybe it isn't anything. Maybe you will live here forever."

"No," Alice said.

"Do you have proof?"

Alice shook her head. "But I never see him, and when I do he doesn't touch me. I told him last weekend that I knew something was up. I really thought he was going to confess, and tell me who she was, and then we could work through it. But he didn't. I'm pregnant, I should tell you that. We weren't going to say anything yet."

Naomi knocked over a saltshaker on the kitchen table. She tried to conceal her surprise by sweeping together the loose grains.

"Left shoulder," Alice said.

"What?"

"Throw the salt over," Alice said. "For luck."

Naomi dropped the grains down her back. "You're *pregnant*?" she asked, trying to make the question friendly.

Alice nodded. "It took me a while to realize," she said. "I was so distracted."

"Do you want a baby?" Naomi asked. No baby would make things much easier. She couldn't come out and say it, but it was true.

"I want a husband," Alice said. "And then a baby. Together. You have no idea what he's like."

"I know a little."

"But you only see him when he's happy at work, or being social at parties," Alice said. "Then he talks. He can talk about *anything,* and people just sit and listen. You've seen it."

"I've been one of them."

"He missed his calling, don't you think? He should have founded a cult. A big house full of barefoot girls sitting cross-legged at his feet. He could go around healing every-one. The laying on of hands. That would make him so happy. Instead he just has me, so he resents me and goes silent. Or he jokes and deflects everything."

"I'm sure that will change."

The electric kettle had boiled and turned itself off, and sat quietly steaming. Alice stared at the porcelain cups on the open shelves, as if they might hold some answer in their pattern of arrangement, then pulled two of them down. She moved easily in her body, and didn't slump like some tall girls; she stood straight and unapologetic. Her hair was short, and right now it looked slept on. "Black tea?" she asked. "Or I have green and peppermint."

"Black is fine."

"Is there anyone—" Alice began, as if casually. "Any of the residents who you think he might—I'm sorry. I shouldn't bring you into this. But you see him more than I do, almost."

"He's a very dedicated doctor."

"Yeah, because his patients all beam at him, and hang on every word." Alice put the tea bags in the cups and poured the water. "Have you noticed the way he keeps his voice really low, sort of half-throttle, especially when he's talk-ing to women? His father does it, too. It's to show they're not trying to be brilliant, never trying. They're *reining* their natural brilliance in, so it doesn't overwhelm us all."

"You don't seem to like him very much," Naomi said.

"I don't, when he's fucking someone else!"

"You don't know that."

"You take milk, right?" Alice went to the refrigerator.

"It doesn't matter."

"I thought he was a genius when I married him," Alice said, pouring milk in the tea. "I thought he was a god. I never questioned anything he did. I did everything he ever wanted me to do, everything I ever *thought* he wanted me to do. I was his slave, because he was a god, and I was just a girl who'd stepped in the way of his godly attention. That he was, you know, *married*, to someone else, and had a baby—that just seemed like a technicality. We were so in love that nothing else mattered. You don't take sugar."

"No."

She brought the tea to the table and Naomi accepted it in silence, thinking about the cup, white porcelain, his coffee.

"The whole soul mates idea," Alice said bitterly, "is really most useful when you're stealing someone's husband. It's not so good when someone might be stealing yours." She paused, looking out the window. "If I knew who it was, I would get down on my knees and I would *beg* her to go away, just go away and leave my family alone."

"Assuming that she exists," Naomi said. She wished she

hadn't come. She hadn't been able to think of an excuse when Alice called, except general exhaustion, which didn't count. And then there was the perverse desire to know what Alice would say.

"For a while I thought it was one of the nurses," Alice said. "Little Mandy. But I don't think it is now."

"Mandy's engaged."

"So? He's married." She paused in thought. "But he would think it was an outdated cliché. Doctors don't really go for nurses anymore. It used to be a way to marry up in the world, for nurses and secretaries. But now doctors go for doctors, lawyers for lawyers. So maybe it's another resident."

"I think you're imagining this."

"I wouldn't imagine it if it didn't seem true," Alice said. "Do you think Max is cheating on you?"

Naomi hesitated. She had told her husband that she was leaving him, with the understanding that Alice would simultaneously—or at least soon—be told the same thing. It had been a difficult week. "No," she said.

"Because he's *not* cheating," Alice said. "You see, I'm not insane, or stupid. Besides, you're beautiful, and you're a doctor, for God's sake, and you aren't pregnant and sick every morning."

"I'm sure he loves you."

"We were so happy," Alice said. "I gave up my job and my friends and my whole life to move with him here, and

I didn't care. It was such a perfect residency, in such a cool place, and the houses were so cheap—we could *never* have bought this house in L.A. I loved being a doctor's wife in a place that needs doctors, and I was going to have his brilliant, beautiful baby. I was so happy to do all of that, so blissed out on it all. And now it's fucked."

"You don't know that."

"I do," she said. "He's never used this kitchen. He learned how to cook as a kid because his family had a bad cook, and he used to show off for me. So I made him this kitchen, and got the right burners, the right hood—and he doesn't cook anymore."

Naomi had been cooked for, in a motel with a kitchenette, on crappy electric burners. Just eggs, but spectacular eggs, with capers and Raclette. He had fed her yellow forkfuls, hot and salty and runny with melted cheese. He said she had to eat well, if she was going to keep up her schedule *and* these antics. "He's so busy," she said now.

"But cooking was his *thing*."

The phone rang, and Alice stood from the table, lifting her hips forward as if her center of gravity had changed, though she wasn't showing yet. Naomi wondered if she was doing it deliberately, to look like a woman who couldn't be left.

Alice rubbed her red eyes and peered at the screen on the cordless phone. "It's him," she said, and Naomi's heart skipped. It rang again, and Alice picked up.

"Hi," she said. "Sure. I'm just here with Naomi." She made a funny, eye-rolling face at whatever he said. "Why shouldn't she be? We're having tea. That's what women do." She paused. "No, everything's fine. I mean, except, you know, that my life is falling apart. I told her a little bit about that. I hope you don't mind. How was the gym?" There was another pause. "Okay, we'll see you soon, then." She put the phone back in the charger. "He's coming home. Do you think he's been fucking her?"

"I should go," Naomi said. The image of the adorable nurse, Mandy, flashed through her mind, but that was ridiculous.

"No, stay," Alice said, trying to smooth her hair, with no effect. "You'll be a good buffer. We don't have any way of not fighting anymore. We used to do this thing—we would dance a little two-step, to make up, any time we had a disagreement. We did it in the grocery store, and at people's houses. They must have thought it was so obnoxious. But the dancing dissolved the fight, it meant we could never stay mad. I loved him so much."

"Do you still love him?"

"I do," she said. "Beyond reason. I even called his ex-wife. Isn't that pathetic? I wanted to know if he was like this—then."

"What did she say?"

"She wasn't very compassionate—I mean, obviously. I

don't know what I was thinking. She asked me if I thought I was so special that I could change him, and make him faithful. She said she was still breast-feeding their baby when he left her, so she had trouble feeling very sorry for me. And she said he's a pathological narcissist, and would leave whenever he felt like it. Do you think he's a pathological narcissist?"

"I don't know. I don't think so."

"She said at least she had the excuse that she was really young when she met him, and he hadn't abandoned any wives yet, and she wished me luck."

Naomi said nothing.

"So, that worked out well," Alice said. "That was a brilliant phone call to make. I wish I could get her to talk to the new girl."

There was another pause, and Naomi began to sweat with the idea that Alice was playing a deep game. Alice *knew*, and had been batting her around like a trapped mouse. "I really should go," Naomi said.

"No, he likes you," Alice said. "Please stay. He'll be friendly and it will help me. It's such hell when we're alone. You can tell me what you think."

"Alice—" she said.

The door in the front hallway opened. "Hello!" he called, and Naomi felt as if a guitar string in her lower abdomen had just been plucked, and left to vibrate, by the sound of his voice. She believed these responses were biological tricks to propagate the species, but that didn't make them lose their power. She had never felt that way when her husband spoke, though he was a good and decent man.

"Alice," she said again, but Alice was looking toward the kitchen door, like a faithful retriever with her messy hair and her red nose, waiting for her master to appear.

They heard keys drop on a table in the hall, and then he came to the kitchen doorway in gym clothes with snow in his hair. He was so beautiful, and so spoiled. Alice had a look of pure adoration on her face. Of course she didn't know. Naomi thought the pounding of her own heart must be visible through her sweater.

"Hello, ladies," he said. "I won't kiss you, I'm covered in sweat."

His wife tried to put her arms around him.

"No really," he said. "I'm disgusting."

Alice dropped her hands to her thighs as if she had never really expected contact. "You *are* disgusting," she said. "We were just talking about that. That was the topic of the afternoon, in fact."

He smiled. "I'm the leading expert. I could give a guest lecture."

"Why don't you?" his wife asked. "It would be so— edifying."

He patted his pockets. "No notes."

"Oh, just wing it."

"I'm sure you have the salient facts down."

"Actually, we don't," Alice said. "That's exactly what we don't have."

"Why don't you just *tell* her?" Naomi heard herself say. She had meant to keep her mouth shut, but she couldn't stand to watch the two of them banter obliquely about what was now her life: the life she had plunged willingly, headlong into.

He turned to look at Naomi without hurry, his gaze like a police searchlight, taking its time because it had time. It found her in the shadows, casing his house.

"Naomi's right," his wife said. "She's an objective party. We should listen to her advice."

He smiled. It wasn't an unpleasant smile, but it wasn't private, either—not wolfish, not adoring, not wistful. He was being Alice's husband, confronted in his own kitchen, with nothing to hide. She shouldn't have come. "Hello, Naomi," he said. "How's Max?"

"Fine," she lied. Her husband was not as forgiving as Alice. Max had high expectations of other people, and didn't care much for compromise or moral ambiguity. When she married him, this quality had seemed passionate and decisive, but now it seemed harsh. He had trusted her, and now he didn't, and wouldn't again.

Alice reached out to brush her husband's snow-damp hair from his face, but he was still looking at Naomi.

"Who was it who said that marriage is a long struggle for moral advantage?" he asked.

"Someone bitter," Naomi said. "It shouldn't be. It doesn't have to be."

"As I was driving back here from the gym," he said, as if beginning his lecture, "I was thinking about the time I did summer stock at a theater in Colorado, because my older sister was doing it and it seemed like a way to meet girls. And how everyone was isolated, and thrown together in a place they wouldn't be otherwise, and nervous energy became sexual energy. There was friction, and suspicion about who was doing what with whom, and some of it was founded."

"I told her we're having a baby," Alice said.

"You told her we're having a baby," he repeated.

Naomi watched him: his strong hands, the pained look on his face. He had the intelligence that physically beautiful people have, because other people confide in them, but he had real intelligence, too. It was irresistible, even when he was acting indefensibly, as he was now.

"Why don't you just *tell* me," Alice said, "what's going on?"

He opened the refrigerator, pulled out a large bottle of reddish sports drink, and drank from it. Naomi thought she could see him trying to decide what kind of man he was, or what kind he might seem to be. He screwed the cap back on.

"Nothing's going on."

"He always says that," his wife said.

"Nothing?" Naomi asked.

"Nothing," he said, putting the plastic bottle back and closing the fridge. "Except that we're having a baby."

"A *baby*," Alice said plaintively, and she reached for him again. This time he conceded, and took his wife in his sweaty, sweatshirted arms, and they started to dance. He steered her toward the refrigerator with a little hitch in their glide, then toward the dishwasher. She looked as pleased as a child as he spun her around and brought her back in. Then they headed back across the kitchen floor as if they had always been dancing like this, and always would be, and anything else was only a vivid hallucination.

Naomi gathered her coat and edged past them, slipping out through the dining room and down the hall. They ignored her and danced on. She struggled to put her coat on, with clumsy hands. His car keys were on the hall table, where she had listened to them drop as if there were no other sound in the world. She thought of taking them, or of keying some furious message into the gleaming varnish of the table, but that would get her no closer to what she wanted. Also on the table was a black-and-white close-up in a pewter frame of the devastating toddler who could only be his son. Alice's stepson. The boy had loose, dark curls and his father's sleepy look, and he seemed, for such a small child, frightfully knowing. His father was still steering Alice around the kitchen.

Naomi saw how reckless it had been to fall so hard, but it was already done. She was a careful, methodical person in the rest of her life, and she tried to think clearly. She understood, better than Alice did, what he was doing. He was acting like the man he wanted to be, in hopes that he could become it. He would keep acting until he couldn't stand it anymore, and then he would be the man he was. It would happen soon, and then he would need her. The thought gave her some comfort.

She went outside and stood on the step, thinking that she would never get used to unlocked houses, or to snow in September. She thought it might be true that everything had happened because life felt so unreal here—the strange isolation, the long hours, the lack of sleep—that a new life with a new man seemed possible. But it did seem possible.

His car, a beat-up old station wagon that suited his self-deprecation, was parked on the street. She had meant to walk home, but to what? His windshield was still wiped of snow. He would come looking for her soon, to tell her she was all that mattered; that seemed very clear. He wasn't going to dance with Alice all night. His car keys were back in the house, but she didn't need them. She was very tired.

There was so little time for sleep, and now this mental confusion. She opened the unlocked passenger door and got
inside, where it was still warm and smelled of him, and she
rolled the seat back as far as it would go, to sleep and wait.

THE GIRLFRIEND

THE GIRL SAT in one of the mismatched upholstered chairs in the hotel room, and Leo sat in the other, where he'd waited for her to arrive. The window looked out on a courtyard, but the heavy curtains were closed. The girl didn't seem to mind. Leo was still startled that she had come. Finding her ahead of him in line at the sandwich bar near the courthouse, he had asked her to meet him, convinced she'd say no. Or not show. There wasn't much in it for her. But here she was.

"So," Leo said.

"So." She tugged her black skirt so it hung farther over her crossed legs.

"Where did you first meet him?" He wanted to get to the point, but carefully, afraid he might bore her or scare her away.

"At a party."

The black skirt had a pointy, uneven hem, and she wore it with a blue Levi's jacket and black flip-flops. Her hair was streaked dark and light, and her eyes were outlined in black. Montana Goth, he had come to think of it. It wasn't real Goth; her lips were glossed pink.

"What kind of party?" he asked.

"Just some keg, at a house."

"Was it a high school party? Why was he there?"

"He knew the kids who were having it."

He imagined Troy Grayling in a dark room full of teen-agers, sipping cheap beer from a plastic cup.

"How old were you then?" he asked. He felt himself slipping into the rhythms of the courtroom. He did it with his wife, Helen, too, caught himself grilling her, after a day watching the trial. He cross-examined waiters when they went to dinner. Helen was back at their hotel now, reading a novel, thinking he had gone to swim at the university pool.

"Fifteen, I guess," she said.

She was eighteen now, he knew. Troy Grayling, who had killed Leo's daughter, was twenty-four. The case had taken almost two years to come to trial. The trial took two weeks, and the jury had returned a guilty verdict the day before. Leo and Helen had been in the Missoula court-room every day, and it had been harrowing. Each morning in the gallery, confronted with the blank, mildly surprised look on Troy Grayling's face, Leo thought about charging the defense table and prying the young man's eyeballs out of his skull with a ballpoint pen. Or of bringing a knife in Helen's expensive handbag, which no one ever searched, to draw across Grayling's throat: the satisfying pop of the trachea, the sudden flow of blood. No conviction could be satisfying like that. He had touched his own throat during the testimony, feeling for the right spot.

But this girl, Sasha, had been a child when she met Grayling; he tried to remember that.

"How old were you when you first slept with him?" he asked.

"Fifteen," she said.

"Was he the first?"

There was a pause. "Yes," she said. It sounded provisional, and he wondered about her childhood.

"Did he seem dangerous to you? Back then?"

She pulled one foot up on the chair, hugging her knee—the skirt was long and loose enough for that—and considered the question while pulling on her darkly polished toes. It was a childish gesture, not a seductive one. "A little bit," she said. "Not in a bad way."

"It was a good kind of danger?"

"I mean, that's just how Troy was."

Leo blinked, and forced himself to breathe.

He had spoken to his daughter the night she disappeared. It was late in Manhattan, and would have been dark in the wooded canyon outside Missoula, where Emily was house-sitting. She was studying forestry at the University of Montana and had been telling him about her fieldwork, which she loved, when she stopped abruptly and made a funny noise, then said, "Give Angela my love," and hung up. Leo hesitated, called back to no answer, and then called the Missoula police. He didn't know anyone named Angela. It had to be a code: Emily was being told to act natural and get off the phone. He spent some time describing the problem to the dispatcher, and then searching his e-mail inbox for the house address Emily had sent. When the police arrived in the canyon, the house was empty. There was a cut window screen and a full cup of cold tea by the phone, no sign of struggle. They never found the knife, and Leo guessed it was at the bottom of the river that drifted through town. A pair of hikers found Emily's body in a disused railroad tunnel in the mountains. It had been a bad moment when the DA showed the photographs in court. Leo had seen the photos before, but not projected on a six-foot screen. Troy Grayling was the only suspect, with a DNA match, but he had never confessed. He said he had been fishing near Whitefish, two hours north, on the night she was taken. His brother and his parents swore it was true. Leo had quit his job after Emily's death so he could give his full attention to the case, and now it was over, but questions remained unanswered.

Lying awake at night, Leo had gone over the decisions that might have led to a different outcome. If he had objected to Emily's house-sitting in a remote house. If he had tried to keep her on the East Coast for college. If they hadn't sent her at fifteen to the outdoor course in Wyoming that convinced her to want bigness, ruralness, westernness. Leo designed sky-blocking office buildings for a living, and wondered if forestry was a direct challenge to him. But he had loved her adventurousness, amazed that he and quiet Helen, who taught fourth grade in a private school, could produce such a fearless girl.

He had argued with Emily about her choices, to test her resolve, but her gray eyes would only get solemn and sure, and her chin would lift stubbornly. Her favorite book at seven had been *The Lorax*, Dr. Seuss on environmental ruin and corporate greed: "I am the Lorax. I speak for the trees. I speak for the trees, for the trees have no tongues." She had read it in their apartment in Chelsea, with its little square of garden. The chopped trees in the book had triggered in her a fierce indignation and fear for the planet. Even as a child she wanted vast forests, not gardens.

She was their only child, born when he and Helen were

both in their thirties, and they had been happy with one. He wondered now if that had been a mistake, but it was hard to imagine other children. Emily was so particular and real to him, still. The way her hair curled around her small ears, the faces she made at his jokes, her breathless laugh. When she was in high school, a man tried to pull her off her bicycle, and Emily had roared at him, pushing him away, and ridden home. She had described the scene in the kitchen, crying and shaking and laughing at the sound she had made, trying to imitate it with all the adrenaline gone. She was slight but very strong. He wondered why she hadn't fought off Troy Grayling, and guessed the man had surprised her. She had been talking on the phone, and then the knife was at her throat. There were marks there, where he hadn't cut her deeply but had held the blade against the skin. Grayling must have whispered to her to get off the phone as if nothing was wrong, and she must have believed he would kill her if she didn't. But she was clever, and sent her father a signal, knowing he would understand.

The Goth girl was looking at him, waiting. What had she said? *That's just how Troy was.* He tried to pretend that this statement could be reasonable. "What do you mean, that's how he was?"

The girl shrugged. "He had an edge."

"Is that what you call it?"

"He didn't *do* anything," she said, but she watched him

for information about her performance. It was an infantile expression: a child's attempt at lying.

"What about the DNA match?" he asked.

"He was framed by the cops." She threw the words away, bored by them already. "Why did you ask me to a hotel room?"

"To talk in private."

"I thought maybe you wanted to fuck me." Again the unguarded, waiting gaze.

He coughed in surprise. "No."

"Didn't you think about it?"

He hadn't. He had watched her testimony and felt only horror at her loyalty to Troy Grayling, her stonewalling of the DA, but he had hoped to find a way through to her. He had, after all, some experience with teenage girls. Now she lazily pulled off her jean jacket and he watched, frozen, as she crossed to him and put her hands on the arms of his chair, leaning so close he could smell her sweet powdery scent. Her features were immature and undefined under her makeup, and her black tank top hung loose, revealing small breasts in a black bra. Her knees bumped against his.

"But you want to," she said, playing at grown-up seduction. "And I could use the money."

He made himself stern and distant. "Sit down," he said. "I'm not giving you money. I don't want sex. I just have questions I want to ask you."

She sighed, and stood, and flopped down in her own chair again. "Twenty dollars a question."

"I'm not paying you," he said. "I think you owe me the truth."

"I don't owe you shit."

"You shouldn't talk like that."

She laughed and rolled her eyes. "Okay, *Dad*."

The word made his stomach flip. He tried to focus on the questions that had made him approach her in the first place. He was within reach of the information he craved. He just had to find a way through this disorderly adolescent mind. "Did Troy know my daughter?" he asked. "I'm not trying to get you in trouble. I just want to know."

She said nothing.

"If they *had* known each other, how might they have met?"

She sighed, and looked around the dim room.

"Sasha," he said. "Did he know Emily?"

"I dunno."

"But it's possible?"

"Missoula's not huge or anything."

"Had he seen her?"

"Stop asking me!"

"Tell me about him. What does he like to do?"

She thought about it. "He plays drums," she said. "He's awesome at pool. He ran track in high school, and he still likes running, 'cause it calms him down."

"Where did he run?"

"On the river trail, or at the track."

"Which track?"

She hesitated. "The Grizzly one," she said, her eyes locked to his.

Leo forced himself not to react, to stay quiet. Emily had run at the university track. Slight Emily in running tights, on the rubbery track in the clear mountain air. She had a loping, easy stride, and had to sprint to break a sweat. Would Grayling have fallen in beside her? Struck up a conversation?

"So he'd seen her," Leo said. "Did he talk to you about it?"

"No."

"But you know he'd seen her."

"No."

She had wanted to tell him, clearly. Now was she changing her mind?

"I won't get you in trouble," he said. "They already have a conviction. It's just between you and me."

"Fuck off."

"Did he talk to you about her? Did you think he would do something?"

"No!"

"Were you jealous?"

She said nothing.

"You were!" He was on to something, lifting the edge.

"He already had *me*," she said, her voice high and strained.

It took him a second to get his head around this. "What do you mean, he had you?"

"I mean, why did he need *her*?"

"He raped and killed her," he said. "You wanted to be his girl to rape and kill?"

She hesitated. "He wasn't going to hurt her."

There was a silence in the room that seemed to roar in his ears.

"How do you know that?" he asked.

She blushed furiously. "I just know."

He tried to follow this. "Did he rape you?"

She glowered at him, and he knew he was right. He felt the excitement of the chase, of the discovery.

"Did he the first time?" he asked. "Or was that his thing, did you pretend?"

She looked like she might cry. Why hadn't the cops gotten to this? The DA? But the DA was just a kid. And maybe it wouldn't have helped the case, which he had won with what he had.

"So you were jealous of Emily," Leo said, "because Troy had seen her and wanted her. Had you met her, too?"

She shook her head.

"*How* could he kidnap someone else, when he had you, is that it?"

"Why are you *doing* this to me?" she whined.

He was up out of his chair, and had grabbed her by the shoulders. He could tolerate anything except her acting like a victim. "Your boyfriend killed my daughter," he said, close to her face. "Do you understand? There's nothing I can do to you to match that. You encouraged him, and you lied for him in court. You have no heart, you're rotting. Do you see that?"

She was crying.

"Stop *crying!*" He shook her, and threw her back against her flowered chair. She winced, though he hadn't hurt her. The chairs were soft. She curled up against the upholstery and watched him, like an animal waiting to make her next move.

He went into the bathroom, regretting his violence, and sat on the closed toilet lid. The loose end of the toilet paper was folded in a neat triangle, unused. He checked that his wallet was in his pocket, that he had left nothing of his in the room with the girl. He had to keep his guard up. At fifty-three he felt himself an innocent, out of his depth. He should have flown home with Helen the moment the trial ended, and he would have, if he had anything to go back to. Work had been his way of making order: drafting something out of nothing, finding practical solutions. Since Emily's death, the world seemed all chaos and accident. Helen managed to console herself with a hardy, low-level feeling about energy in the universe, but Leo had been deformed by grief, his thoughts of the future shaped only by what they had lost.

He realized Helen would expect him soon, smelling of chlorine from the pool. He took the box of Kleenex out to the girl, and she was still there, amazingly. But maybe he hadn't been gone long. It was hard to gauge time. She blew her nose, her smudged eyes never leaving him. He sat down in his chair.

"What will you do now?" he asked. "Will you go to college?"

She shrugged, folding a tissue around her wet snot. "I can't afford it."

"People work their way through. Have you talked to your guidance counselors?"

She smirked. "They only care about the rich kids and the smart kids," she said. "The rest of us are supposed to get pregnant or married." She was delivering a line she had heard somewhere. She pulled her foot up on the chair again, but more carelessly this time; he caught a length of pale thigh and white panties as she did it. White underwear under all the black. He thought she really would fuck him, right there on the double bed, for very little money. He didn't want to feel protective, he wanted still to hate her, but if she was going to proposition strange, unhappy men, things were going to go badly.

"You have to be more careful," he said.

"Of what?"

"Things like this, like coming to meet me. And men like Troy Grayling. You have to recognize danger."

"You're not dangerous."

"I could have been. There will be enough danger in your life without you seeking it out."

"Why do you care?"

"I don't," he said. "I don't even like you. But I don't see where you're going to get any other concern or advice, so you should take mine. Think about the future. Make some plans."

But Sasha already had a plan, at least a short-term one, and when she spoke, he realized why she had stayed. "I can call the police," she said. "I'll tell them you tried to rape me."

"*What?*"

"I'll tell them you beat me up. You almost did."

"I shook you, once."

"I can give myself bruises."

He felt a surge of panic. He should have seen this coming. "For what, for money?" he said, the anger choking his voice. "You just *try* it. You've already committed perjury, and could go to prison. Do you understand that?"

Her eyes widened slightly with fear, and he thought he had finally struck home. She was right to be scared. He'd show her what an expensive lawyer looked like—a whole team of expensive lawyers, no newly minted DAs.

"Prison," he said, brandishing the word like a stick, since it had worked. "A women's prison. A double cell. You think high school girls are mean? You just *wait*."

She bit her lip, contemplating him, if that sullen glower could be called contemplative. He had the wild thought that if he did fuck her, he could control her. And if he could control one small part of the situation, he might come out the other side a man who could live with himself, a man who could sleep. Or he might destroy what life he had left. He felt locked with her, in the silence, unable to find the next move. Then Sasha found it.

"You want to know what happened?" she asked.

He paused in surprise. "Yes," he said. "Yes. I do."

"You can't tell anyone."

"I promise."

"Troy didn't mean to hurt her."

He sat waiting, feeling very still. He was aware of the size of the room, the distance of the walls.

"He took her somewhere," she said. "I don't know where. And then he was driving her back to that house. I didn't know anything about it. I really didn't." She stopped.

"Go on," he said.

"She was fine, and Troy was bringing her home. But then he saw the cop cars outside her house and got scared."

The chill of this information settled on him. "You're lying."

"You wanted to know."

"You're lying." She knew Leo was the reason the cop cars were there, that he had called them, and she was trying to punish him.

"No," she said.

"So he saw the cop cars, but they didn't see him."

"You can't tell anyone," she said. "They're already locking him up. You promise?"

"I promise. He saw the cop cars. He had raped her at this point? Somewhere else?" He tasted acid in his throat and felt his mind floating above his body, to the right.

She nodded.

"Where did he take her? Why didn't he stay at her house?"

"I dunno."

"But he wasn't planning to kill her."

She shook her head.

"He saw the cars and he got scared."

She nodded again, and he thought a look of sorrow passed over her face. She was telling the truth.

"And then he took her away and killed her."

She said nothing.

He heard his voice rise in anger. "Did he think that if he took her home alive, she wouldn't identify him?" he half shouted. "What did he think?"

"I don't know," she whispered.

"And you're still this *fuckhead* killer's girlfriend?" He wanted to strike her for her pathetic lack of imagination. He thought suddenly that this was the kind of loyalty that Troy Grayling had expected from Emily—Sasha had led him to expect it. We'll play at rape, I'll drop you at home, it will be our secret. Leo also knew, from his floating perspective, that his anger with her was nothing compared to the reckoning with himself that would come later, for the rest of his life. He had cracked Emily's code, he had called the cops, and he had killed her.

He imagined telling Helen what he knew, but his mind went blank with fear. He thought he could smell the anger and wretchedness on his body, coming from his damp armpits, and he wished he had gone to the pool, where now he would smell like bleach and know nothing. He thought fleetingly that if they had never had a child, none of this could have happened.

The girl blew her nose again, nervously triumphant, now that she had played her card and won. She took another tissue and ran it under her eyes to tidy the black smear of her makeup. He had never stood a chance against this budding psychopath. He had tried to give her college advice, for God's sake. He had to get out of the room. It was like the urgency of nausea; he felt sick with closeness and regret.

"I have to leave now," he said. "You do, too. Get your bag."

"I told you what you wanted," she said, immovable,

waiting for her compensation. He couldn't drag her out; he couldn't be seen with a teenager in ruined makeup. But he wanted her gone. He pulled out his wallet, which had six twenties in it.

"Here," he said. He shoved the bills into her handbag. "That's all I have. Get out. And try not to draw attention." He hung the bag on her shoulder and pushed her out the door.

When she was gone, his legs gave out, and he had to sit down on the bed. He never should have come. Ignorance had been bad, but it had been infinitely better than this. He sat until he thought his legs would hold him, and then he went to the lobby, which was quiet in the middle of the afternoon. He dropped the key at the desk and thanked the clerk, who asked him to sign the bill. The sky outside was vast and cloudless blue and he squinted against it. No policemen came to arrest him, no girl was waiting with bruises on her arms. He was going to be left alone, to try to explain to Helen about the girl, and what she had told him.

He put on his sunglasses. He had thought his faith in order was gone, but it wasn't true. He had sought consolation in knowing and arranging the facts. He wanted a story and he got one. His daughter had stumbled into danger, and he had tried to fix things and got it wrong. And now she was dead. It was a story with a beginning, a middle, and an end, with cause and effect.

The pain was still settling in, making its home in his body, in his bones, but he was healthy, in spite of Helen's fears for his heart. There might be decades left for him not to forgive himself. He steadied himself and then started to walk back, with uneven steps, to his wife.

LILIANA

ON A HAZY SUMMER AFTERNOON in Los Angeles, while my wife was at work and our children were napping, I answered the ringing doorbell to find my grandmother, two months dead, standing on the stoop. She gave me a happy smile of self-welcome, then turned and waved to a black car with dark windows that purred at the curb. The car pulled away.

"Liliana," I said.

"Darling!" she said.

She reached for my face, so I bent to be kissed, thinking that the woman I was kissing should be dead, her ashes sealed in an expensive vault. But her lips on my cheek were warm, and she smelled like her old perfume and new wool.

"Are you going to ask me in?" she asked.

I stepped back from the door, and she clicked past me on high heels, carrying a small black handbag. She looked great for eighty-seven, let alone for being dead. Her blond hair still seemed plausible, and she held her face in the alert, wide-eyed attitude in which it looked youngest. Under her coat she wore a black cocktail dress, as if she had come from her own funeral. But there had been no service, yet.

She stopped in the living room. "So this is how you live," she said, surveying the piles of half-read newspapers, the children's small jackets hanging on doorknobs, the stain from a wet glass on the leather couch. She spun to face me, then dropped into the big yellow chair.

"I'm very tired," she said. "They lost my bags."

"Do you know what they're saying?"

"It's all a mistake," she said.

I nodded, and thought about what that might mean. "But," I finally said, "there was an autopsy." I didn't want to offend, and here she was, but there had been an autopsy.

"Some lemonade would be nice," my grandmother said.

I went to the kitchen for a glass of cranberry juice, which was what I had besides the kids' boxes of Juicy Juice, and when I returned, Liliana had slipped off her shoes. The way she took the glass and drained it seemed very corporeal.

"The obituaries are here somewhere," I said, before realizing that they might embarrass her. They were from English papers and they described her impoverished London childhood with a German mother and an English father, and her flight at sixteen to become a cabaret girl in Berlin. She had appeared in two movies under the Nazi studio system, and left for Switzerland in 1939. The articles ran briskly through her marriage to a Swiss industrialist, her brief move to the United States, and the five additional husbands she outlived or discarded. They described her famous parties and her expensive houses, and ended with her death as an aged socialite at her remote house in Spain. Men loved her, and she made efficient use of them. With the only American husband, she had a child—my father—and variously unsuitable nurses and nannies had raised him. My father loathed her, but that wasn't in the obituaries. They mentioned his early death of a brain tumor. He would have hated appearing with his mother in print.

Liliana brushed the suggestion away with one hand. "I've seen them all," she said. "Not a word about what I did for the animals."

"The animals," I said stupidly.

"Not a single mention," she said. "Isn't that rich? I gave them *everything*. And now they don't want to give the money back."

I had tried not to think about the money. There had been so much of it, and it had gone in its breathtaking entirety to the Royal Society for the Prevention of Cruelty to Animals. An apologetic lawyer had told me on the phone that in Spain, two-thirds of an estate had to go to family members—here hope rose in my heart—but that as a British subject, Liliana was exempt from the rule, and I would get nothing. The call left me shaken, off-balance. I didn't see Liliana often. Mina hadn't wanted her money, and I told myself I hadn't counted on it, but that was a lie. The photography magazine I worked for had folded, and we were living on Mina's teaching salary while I took care of the kids and looked for a new job. Even a small inheritance—some forgotten sweepings from the giant pile of cash—would have made such a difference. How much did the dogs and cats really need?

"It's so silly," Liliana said. "My lawyer has been my friend for so long, and he was never on time for a luncheon in his life, but now he sets speed records. He pays the Spanish taxes, and sells my house, and gives away the money. And the RSPCA didn't even write a press release. They're not getting a cent from me next time."

"Next time?"

"When I really die."

"Ah," I said, and again I felt a flutter in my heart, but I also heard Mina's voice saying, *Don't get your hopes up.* Liliana was likely, next time, to leave it all to the Royal Ballet.

"I had friends in Los Angeles," Liliana said, gazing out the window at our weedy backyard. "King Vidor, you knew him?"

"No," I admitted.

"And Darryl Zanuck—who was a pig. Garbo and Chaplin, of course. They're all dead." She sighed for her lost past. "It's so different now. I was here ten years ago, when a few of my friends were still alive, and we went to Trader Vic's. At the very next table, there were *six gay Negroes*. Can you imagine?"

I couldn't tell if she had been thrilled or horrified by the sight. It could have been either. I was going to tell her not to say Negro but instead I asked, "How did you know they were gay?"

She looked at me as if I were simple, with pity. "How is your mother, darling?" she asked.

Since my father's death, my mother had been living in an ashram outside New Delhi. She sent us postcards about how deeply at peace she was, in the land of the caste system and the dowry murder. "She's fine," I said. "She's in India."

"India," Liliana said. "How unpleasant. I hope she has those little hand wipes."

"I'm sure she does," I said. I was sure she didn't.

"Listen, darling," Liliana said. "I don't want to impose, but do you have a room for me?"

I said of course we did. She could have our bedroom, and Mina could sleep with the children. I would sleep on the couch. Liliana's house in Spain had seven guest bedrooms, or eight. A whole guest wing, where plates of fruit from the gardens appeared in the rooms: apricots and fat grapes. I tried to imagine who had bought the place. I told myself it was good I hadn't inherited it. It would rot the children's souls, sap their independence, destroy their work ethic. It was the most wonderful place I had ever spent the night. "I'll just be a minute," I said.

While I stripped the master bed and carried the sheets to the wash, I thought about Jesus and Elvis. People had *wanted* them back, badly, and still did. But who would have willed Liliana back? Even Garbo and Chaplin had stayed gracefully dead, and Liliana had left no movies to love. My wife, whose family is Jewish, says that I tricked her into falling in love with me by withholding my grandmother's Nazi movie past until it was too late, which is entirely true—I'm not an idiot.

When the sheets were agitating in the washer, I found my grandmother curled up in the yellow chair, asleep. Her makeup was simpler than I remembered, her lipstick a little blurred, her face smoothed by surgeons and sleep. She looked like the cabaret girl she had been. Her hands gave her away, their spotted, swollen knuckles impossible to hide with heavy rings. She woke and stretched her arms, smiling.

"Cat nap!" she said.

I sat down and spoke carefully. "I just want to under-stand," I said. "Your lawyer called me from France and said you had drowned in the pool."

Liliana frowned, with her old disdain. "It was my care-taker's wife," she said. "She was wearing my clothes and my jewels, and she was drunk. She fell in."

"But the caretaker?"

"He thought he was in my will. He fired all the servants and told those idiot country police I had drowned. He was deranged, clearly. I was at a retreat in Bali, where the whole idea was to be out of touch, and it worked! It was madness on everyone's part."

There was a muffled thumping of small, socked feet in the hall. On her fourth birthday, Bethie had decided she was too old for naps. She would wake from them early, then shake Marcus, who was five but still willing to sleep. The children trundled in, blinking and shy, and looked in confusion at the lady in black in their big yellow chair.

Liliana held her arms out wide. "Hello darlings," she said. "It's your Granny Liliana!"

I had told the children about their great-grandmother's death. Mina said they didn't really understand death yet, but I thought it was important to be direct about these things. We had read a book called *The Tenth Good Thing About Barney*, about a beloved cat who dies and helps make the flowers grow up from the ground. Now my son stood with clasped hands and looked at his dead granny hard, as if enough thinking would make everything clear. Bethie burst into tears.

"Honey," I said, picking her up. "It's okay. She's just come to visit."

"Didn't she die?" Marcus asked me.

"They made a mistake," I said. "She's fine."

Marcus turned his level gaze on the ancient blonde in the living room. "Where are the doggies?" he asked. They had seen a picture of her by a blue swimming pool with three little white Papillons, with oversized ears, and it had made a big impression.

Liliana waved a hand in disgust at the memory. "Oh," she said. "The caretaker drowned them in a sack."

Now it was Marcus's turn to tremble into tears.

"Darling!" Liliana cried, reaching for him. "I'll get new doggies! As soon as I get my money back from the horrible RSPCA!"

Marcus backed away from her, and I gathered my frightened children into my arms on the couch. I told them it was all right. I told Liliana they were still half asleep. We were all sitting that way when Mina came home from work. Her voice in the hallway said, "Babe, I'm too tired to get dinner—" and then she saw us all and stopped. "You're alive," she said to Liliana.

"Of course I am."

"I guess we're not having pizza, then," Mina said.

"Pizza!" the children cried.

"Mina dear," Liliana said, standing to take my wife's hand. "I haven't seen you with this Sapphic haircut. Your children are lovely."

Mina's hair was cut short because she had no time to deal with it, and I thought of it as gamine-like and sexy. "Thank you," Mina said. "You look great. Especially under the circumstances."

"It was all a mistake," Liliana said.

"I see."

"We could go out to dinner, to celebrate," I offered, avoiding my wife's eye. While I was out of work, we had established what we called the New Austerity, and its cardinal prohibition was restaurants.

"Pizza!" the children cried again.

"Pizza would be very nice," my grandmother said.

Forty-five minutes later we were eating on the couch, in front of the TV. Mina had changed into sweatpants and graded papers while she ate. Liliana still wore her black dress. She wanted to watch the news, to see if there was anything about her. She had always, when I knew her, employed a butler, a waiter, a chef, and a couple of housemaids, but she handled the plate on her lap with perfect ease. The children gave her instructions on eating the pizza.

The sight of my children and my grandmother eating together was oddly thrilling. My parents and I had moved abruptly and often, kept late hours, and lived beyond our means. Liliana was only a fraught rumor, and a source of unpredictable gifts. Once I went to a friend's grandmother's house after school and she made buttered saltine crackers, baked in the oven on a metal tray. We sat on a worn green carpet with the hot crackers, careful not to let butter drip through the little holes onto our laps, and we watched *The Brady Bunch* with the grandmother, who told me to call her Nana. The house seemed like a bastion of stability and normality, and I was completely happy there. I had fantasies of my only grandmother inviting me to Spain, to eat buttered saltines.

When I finally did visit Liliana, on a Eurail pass in college, in defiance of my father, we sat in straight-backed chairs at a formal table. Silent servants brought our food, and a candle centerpiece made it difficult to see her across the table. I had arrived in a lull between more interesting guests, just missing an exiled prince, a gossip columnist, and a banker from Zurich who brought his own helicopter. Liliana was tired, and sated with flattery. She treated me like a lover she took for granted. When I asked about her German movies, she grew alert and looked at me shrewdly.

"Let me guess," she said. "Your virtuous father has been calling me a Nazi whore."

I mumbled a vague protest.

"One of the movies was a love story," she said. "The other was a silly musical. I would have done more, if

I could. It was such fun. There was a part in a comedy that I very much wanted, but they had a Bavarian girl with splendid breasts." She mimed the breasts in front of her own. "She would have gone to fat, but at the time she made me look like a little English mouse. So I went back to singing. Then the war came. The Bavarian girl died in the bombing, I heard."

She offered me a chocolate from a plate, and the silent waiter brought tiny cups of espresso. She said, "I was so happy your father was going to be an American. I always envied Americans. Their lives seemed so simple. But that was foolish. I don't mean to put you in the middle, but it's very tiresome, your father's virtue."

I mumbled something again, this time a kind of apology.

"Somewhere I have the musical," she said. "A friend found it for me. You can see it if you like. I'm not terribly good. Now, sweetheart, I'm off to bed."

She kissed me carelessly on the lips and we each went to our bedrooms in the vast silent house. Outside was darkness: dark trees, dark sea in the distance. The next day, Liliana gave me a Betamax tape, and after dinner I watched the movie alone, on a television deep in the house. It was a banal musical about a convent girl in the big city, except that it was in German and therefore ominous and scary. At one point the girl was threatened by a Gypsy. My father had made it sound like *Triumph of the Will*, and maybe it was, if you could understand what they were saying. Liliana had a sweet, clear voice and a fetching smile. I could see why men left their fortunes at her feet.

Years later, when my father died, Liliana—who had by then buried four husbands and divorced two—sent me a thick, cream-colored, black-bordered note of consolation. She gave her regrets for the funeral, and ended with the hope that I had not learned very much either from my father or from her.

Now my own small family, which I had built on the model of buttered saltines in front of the TV, was piled on our secondhand couch with that same distant grandmother. There was nothing about Liliana on the news, of course, but she seemed inclined to watch the sitcom that followed. Marcus and Bethie drew nearer to her as she giggled at the screen. Mina brought out praline ice cream, and soon the children were leaning sticky-fingered against their great-grandmother, one on each side.

"That's what I wanted!" I told Mina in the kitchen. "A normal childhood, a granny to eat ice cream and watch TV with. I wanted it so much."

"Why isn't she dead?"

"It was the caretaker's wife in her clothes."

Mina rinsed a plate. "You have to explain it to me when I'm not so tired," she said.

I made up our queen-sized bed with the clean sheets, and Mina loaned Liliana a nightgown. When everyone was packed off to sleep—Mina in the children's room, to their delight—I lay on the couch and stared at the ceiling, thinking about my grandmother giggling on this couch and holding contests with the children to see who could stretch the mozzarella the longest.

In the morning, after Mina went to work, Liliana announced that she had a car coming and she was taking Marcus and Bethie shopping in Beverly Hills.

"Everything costs a fortune there," I said.

"It's where I used to go."

"The kids don't last long, shopping," I said. "They start to melt down."

"Well," she said, "it's time for them to learn."

I watched the three of them climb into another shiny black town car, and wondered if my grandmother knew about taxis.

"Don't lose my kids," I said. She patted my cheek.

I WENT BACK in the house and shaved close, to get rid of the gray in my beard, for my own morale. It was exhilarating to have a kid-free morning, and I pulled up my résumé on the computer and changed the font. It looked much better. I started moving my accomplishments around.

At noon, though, I started to worry, and thought I should have told my grandmother to call and check in. At one, I made a sandwich and imagined telling Mina that I'd let the kids go off alone with a woman who had never been known for her judgment. At one-thirty, I tried to distract myself by raking leaves in the backyard, and at two, I came inside to find my children in a screaming tussle with a white yapping dog, while my grandmother looked on, beaming.

"What is this?" I asked.

Marcus and Bethie, with their finely tuned receptors for parental opinion, froze. The dog kept whirling and barking, then stopped, confused.

"It's a new doggie!" Liliana said, still beaming.

"Is it yours?" I asked.

"No, darling, it's theirs."

Marcus and Bethie were on the verge of tears now, full of the misgivings they'd ignored at the pet store.

"We can't have a dog, Liliana," I said. "I have to go back to work. There's no one to take care of it."

"*We'll* take care of it!" Marcus said.

"You'll be in school," I reminded him.

My grandmother looked around the living room, as if for the dog-loving servants who might be hiding behind the furniture. She looked back at me, wide-eyed. "Every child should have a dog," she said.

"I'm sure that's true," I said. "We just can't right now."

"But the children are so happy!"

The children did not look happy at all. Here was their great-grandmother, returned from the grave, just to give them an animal they couldn't keep.

"Have they had lunch?" I asked.

"Yes, of course!" Liliana said, then she looked at the children, considering. "No," she said. "Perhaps not. I think someone at the pet store gave them a cookie."

"Let's get lunch," I said. "We'll talk about the dog when Mina gets home."

While I fed the kids, the dog chewed a hole in the seat of the big yellow chair.

"We can just flip it over," I said, trying to be magnanimous, but when I turned over the cushion, there was a hole chewed in the other side. I looked at Liliana, who shrugged.

"I had the same idea," she said.

By the time Mina came home, it had been decided: Bethie was allergic, with angry red welts on her throat and chin and wrists. She was noble and brave, willing to suffer all manner of torture for the still-unnamed dog, but the hives were spreading.

Mina had brought Chinese takeout from the good place, in violation of the New Austerity, and we ate at the kitchen table. Liliana sat archly beside me, her hair tied back with a pale blue ribbon of Bethie's. When I met her eye, she raised her painted eyebrows, as if catching a stranger staring.

Bethie, her neck ringed with hives, was still working the angles. "Is there," she said, "a different doggie I can have?"

"One that won't make her sick?" Marcus asked.

"No, babe," Mina said. "No dog."

They knew that was it: Mina's word was the law. Bethie frowned mournfully at her plum sauce–smeared plate, and her brother shot her a resentful look.

I N THE MORNING, Liliana waited in her black coat, with her handbag packed, for the car service. The children were in the backyard, saying goodbye to the dog: Bethie with socks over her hands and a bandanna tied over her nose and throat.

"I hoped you might stay," I said to Liliana. "The kids are just getting to know you."

"We have your daughter's health to consider," she said primly.

"The pet store might take the dog back."

She looked astonished. "That would be cruel," she said. "He has a home, with me."

"Where will you go?"

"My lawyer found me an apartment in Paris," she said. "He's very contrite. And the RSPCA is beginning to be reasonable. I'll be fine."

I nodded. I had no doubt of that. Even when she was dead she had been fine. Another black car pulled up to the curb, and Liliana stood and clapped her hands. The dog came running through the back door to her heels, as if it had always been hers.

"Come, darling," she said to it. "We're on our way."

The children and I trailed her out and watched as she eased into the car after the dog, swinging her high heels gracefully in.

"Can we come visit the doggie in Spain?" Marcus asked.

She laughed. "I don't even have a house yet," she said. "I'm going to France now. Come give me a kiss."

The children did, and then I did, too, leaning into the car. I smelled her perfume and her wool coat, and the faint staleness of the dress worn three days in a row. The dog climbed into her lap, and she rubbed its ears and cooed at it. Then she smiled her film-star smile at me, squeezed my arm with her elegant, twisted hand, and pointedly let go. I was blocking the car door, holding her up.

"Why did you come here?" I asked, risking annoying her.

She looked startled, and blinked once. "I wanted to see you," she said. "To see how you had grown up."

"And?"

She tilted her head as if to see me better. "Well, you aren't very much like your father, thankfully," she said.

"But you aren't very much like me, either. Maybe there's something your mother isn't telling us."

I could feel my face doing something unattractive. "You think she was cheating on my father?"

"Oh, don't be such a bore," she said. "It was a joke!"

I wanted to be light and flippant, as she was, but I felt cold pass through me. It was like people described the presence of ghosts. Disillusioned with the effect of her gift to the animals, she had come to check out her biological legacy, and decide if I was a worthy heir. I tried to keep the neediness out of my voice, but it wasn't neediness, it was need.

"Will I see you again?" I asked.

"Don't be silly," she said. "I'm not *dying*." She waved to the children, behind me. "Goodbye, darlings."

"Liliana," I said.

"My flight, darling," she said. "I'll write to you soon."

Then she pulled the door closed, and the car slid away from the curb. With my children at my side, I stood watching it cruise toward the end of our block. She wouldn't send for us when she had a new house. She wouldn't be calling for my Social Security number when she wrote her new will. She had appeared on my doorstep only to dismiss me a second time, more decisively now that she had made a careful inspection, and recognized nothing of herself in me. I tried to say, like Mina, *Good riddance*, but I was not as sensible as my wife. I felt a rising anguish in my chest. We hadn't made ourselves as vivid to Liliana as the fate of some unneutered cats. We had failed, even in overtime, and she was gone.

NINE

WHEN VALENTINE WAS NINE, her mother's new lover took them one night to a bonfire the college kids had at the lake. He carried her in her nightgown from the house to his faded red convertible, and put her in the back seat with his son. They parked between two pickup trucks and walked toward the blaze in the dark. The air smelled like woodsmoke, and the students stood in a circle, lit up by the fire, drinking beers and talking. Carlo was the Italian teacher at the college, and some of the students said "Ciao" and laughed and shook his hand, or gave him five. His son, Jake, who was ten, wandered to the other side of the fire. Valentine sat on a patch of grass in her nightgown, still sleepy.

"College was the best time," Carlo said, hugging her mother around the waist. "It never gets any better."

He hadn't yet spent a night at their house. Valentine's mother said he was the dangerous kind of handsome, and that his name was really just Charles. He would look hard at the person he was talking to, as if what they were saying was supremely important, then lose interest and drop the conversation. His son, Jake, was beautiful, everyone said so.

Across the fire, Jake was talking to a ponytailed college girl, both of them sitting cross-legged on the ground. Their faces were rosy orange in the firelight, with the dark water of the lake behind them. Jake made the older girl laugh, and she put a hand on his cheek. Valentine watched them. Her mother's last boyfriend had a daughter, who asked if Valentine really liked her mother, and why her bedroom was so small. The girl asked what she called her *unit*—what word she used—and laughed when Valentine didn't know what she meant.

"Are you bored, honey?" her mother asked.

Valentine shook her head, stretching her nightgown tight over her knees.

Carlo drove them home, and in the back seat Valentine fell asleep. In the morning she came out of her room to find Jake awake under blankets on the couch. She opened her mother's door, and Carlo was in her mother's bed. He lifted his head from the pillow.

"There's money in my jeans," he said. "Two maple bars and a newspaper for me. Gwen?"

"I'll make breakfast," her mother said, but she didn't get up. Her hair spilled out on the pillow, and her shoulder was bare. She usually wore her hair up and a nightgown.

"The kids are going for breakfast," Carlo said. "And how about knocking next time."

On the walk to the store, Valentine had to run in skipping steps to keep up with Jake. He knew how to order at the pastry counter, and he added an apple fritter for himself. He knew which newspaper to buy. Valentine watched him pay, and thought of the girl touching his face.

Back at the house, they knocked on the bedroom door. Valentine's mother came out in a robe and went to make coffee. Jake and Valentine climbed over the bedcovers with the bag of maple bars and the newspaper. Carlo pulled Valentine close, squeezed her shoulders and spoke into her hair.

"Sorry I said that about knocking," he said. "Your mom just needs her privacy. I want us all to be friends."

Jake didn't look in their direction, but ate his apple fritter, inspecting the inside between bites.

When they had gone, Valentine's mother pulled the covers off the bed. She looked dreamy and happy; she wore lace underwear under her untied bathrobe and her hair was brushed.

"He said I have wonderful cleavage," she said. "Do you know what that is?"

"No."

"It's the space between your breasts."

Valentine thought about this information, and about the word. Her mother's breasts were small, compared to other women's, and separated by several inches of breastbone that might have been Valentine's own.

"He said it was surprising that I didn't shave under my arms," her mother said, shaking a pillow out of its case. "So I shaved." She laughed. "So much for my feminist principles. I kind of like it, though. I told him I didn't think Italian women shaved, but he said they did. I'm not sure he's right. They're more natural in Europe." She shook the other pillow out, and dropped the pillowcase on the floor. "So what did you think of Jake?"

"I don't know."

"I think Carlo's a good father."

Valentine tried, as she sometimes did, to remember her own father living in the house. He had been too tall for the overhead light fixture in the kitchen, and swore when he bumped his head but never took the fixture down. Her parents had fought, but that was just part of life. Then he was gone, living in California. When Valentine asked why he had moved so far away, her mother sat down on the couch to answer. She said that they just couldn't stay in the same town, divorced. His pull on her was too strong, and he couldn't stand her having a new relationship, so neither of them would have been happy. When Valentine asked her father the same question on the phone, he said, "I had an important job to do in California." Then he asked what her mother said about it. Valentine said she didn't know. For a while, at night, she would hear the phone ring and then her mother crying, but that had stopped.

Her mother bundled up the sheets, and carried them past Valentine into the kitchen.

THERE FOLLOWED a difficult period, as Gwen ran through her divorce settlement. She polished her wedding silver to have it appraised, but came home from the jeweler's crying, unwilling to sell it. She was happy in the mornings after Carlo stayed, but whatever he did wore off, and she was miserable again. They ate from her wedding china, with the silver scrollwork around the edges, because those were the only plates. She grew vegetables to sell to a local organic café, and they ate what was left. When Valentine found a steamed white worm on her broccoli, her mother said, "It's from the garden."

"It's a *worm*."

"Just take it off."

"It's gross."

"I ate my broccoli already," her mother said, smiling wanly, making a joke. "At least you found your worm first."

"I don't want to eat things from the garden anymore."

Her mother stared at her, looking lost. Then she stood, dropped her plate in the sink, and shut her bedroom door.

Summer days, Valentine went to the public library downtown. She sat in the empty children's section, reading comic books: *The Incredible Hulk*, and the *Archie and Veronicas* her mother said were sexist. A bearded man in a jean jacket sometimes sat close to her, and brushed against her once as she leaned over a table, reading. The librarian came over and asked him to leave. After that, Valentine would glance around the library, to see if he was there. She looked forward to school starting in the fall.

ONE DAY SHE WALKED home to find Carlo stalking back and forth across the living room, and her mother sitting on the couch. He was angry.

"Rich brats," he said. "It's worse in summer school. Everyone indulges them."

"Did you sleep with one of them?" her mother asked.

"No!" he said. "Jesus."

"What did you do?"

"I gave them the grades they deserved. I wouldn't take late papers. They complained to the fucking dean."

"They can't fire you for grades."

"Maybe I yelled a little."

"Is there some kind of probation?"

"I was already on that."

"Jake's outside, baby," her mother said to her.

She found Jake bouncing a volleyball on his knee, on the other side of the big pine tree. The sun lit up his dark hair, and Valentine wanted to touch it, he was so beautiful. She wondered if Jake were the dangerous kind of handsome, if that was why she had a nervous feeling in her chest.

"Is he still mad?" Jake asked.

She nodded.

"He made dinner for some students and they got drunk," he said. "One hit a tree in her car. Angie. She's okay, though."

"Does my mom know?"

"She doesn't know *anything*." Jake kicked the volleyball into the lilacs, and Valentine watched it disappear. "What's there to do here?" he asked.

"We can go up on the roof."

The old maple tree was easy to climb, and its branches stretched out over Valentine's bedroom. There were maple seeds scattered on the flat roofing, and she showed Jake how to spin the dried ones like helicopters to the ground.

"This is so cool!" Jake said, running up to the roof's peak and leaping over it, arms in the air, then skidding down on his rubber-soled Vans to where the asphalt shingles flattened out again.

"We're not supposed to be up here," Valentine said. "There are live wires."

Jake spoke to the lines that ran over their heads. "General and Mrs. Electric!" he said. "We want permission to be on the roof!"

Valentine sat on her heels on the incline, watching him act out all the parts—the general barking orders, long-suffering Mrs. Electric, Jake the boy who had come to play on the roof—and she wished she could make up things like that. He kept going until his father yelled, "Jake!" from below.

Then Jake's face grew solemn, and they climbed in silence down the tree.

Gwen said, "There are live wires up there," and Jake sneaked Valentine a look. Carlo wasn't speaking to anyone. With Jake in the car, he drove away too fast down the gravel alleyway.

T HEY READ about the accident in the newspaper. Angela Ellberg, twenty-one, had been charged with DUI. The instructor who provided the alcohol, Charles Gregory—that was Carlo—had been fired. Valentine's mother was furious, red-faced and crying.

"Why didn't he tell me?" she demanded.

Valentine thought of Jake saying her mother didn't know *anything*.

Carlo and Jake came to the house that night with two bottles of red wine and a sack of groceries. Gwen stopped them at the door. "Why didn't you tell me?" she asked.

"The college wanted to keep it a secret," Carlo said. "They asked me not to tell."

"But I listened to you talk about *grades*!"

"I'm sorry," Carlo said. "I should have told you. Can I come in?" He walked past them with the groceries. Jake sidled over to the stereo to look at the records. Valentine followed her mother and Carlo into the kitchen.

"What are you going to do?" Gwen asked.

Carlo picked Valentine up and spun her around, saying, *"O donna di virtù, beata e bella, loda di Dio vera!"*

"Please speak English," Gwen said.

"Instead of Dante?" he asked. "I like your hair like that, Val."

Valentine touched her braids, and he put her down and started unpacking the groceries.

"I'm filing a lawsuit," he said. "They should never have fired me. I'm going to rake them over the proverbial coals."

Her mother frowned at the filmy plastic produce bags on the counter, and Valentine knew she was thinking that she already had lettuce and good tomatoes, her own. "A lawsuit for what?"

"Wrongful termination."

"Who's Angela Ellberg?"

"My best student. I had no idea she was drunk."

"You gave them alcohol."

"A glass of wine," Carlo said. "Anyone who got an *A* on the Italian midterm got an Italian dinner. This is not a crime. They were all of age. Angie has a bump on her head and a scratch on her arm, and it's her own damn fault. They were drinking *before*."

"You could have asked me to the dinner."

"Oh, boy," Carlo said. He set a can of tomato paste on the counter. "Are you mad because you disapprove of the event, or because you weren't invited?"

Valentine's mother said nothing.

"I thought it would be more of a drinking-type social thing if you were there," he said. "I was trying—God help me—to be appropriate. Now close your eyes."

She stared at him a minute, and then did close her eyes, and he took a necklace of tiny dark-red beads from his pocket and hooked it around her neck.

"Look, I'm sorry," he said. "I know this is an embarrassing mess. That looks nice."

She went to look in the bathroom mirror, and Carlo gave Valentine a funny, apologetic smile and shrugged. Her mother came back and kissed him, and he opened a bottle of wine and started to cook. He was short enough for the low ceiling, and never hit his head on the light.

They put out the china plates for dinner, and Carlo added two more wineglasses, pouring some for Jake and Valentine.

"Carlo, please," Gwen said.

"I refuse to pretend it's an evil," he said. "Kids drink it in Italy from their baby bottles. I've given them a tiny bit. Now sit down and *mangia, mangia*. How is it?"

"Aside from the tomatoes?"

"You haven't even tried them yet. Valentine, what do you think?"

Valentine glanced at her mother. The tomatoes didn't have worms. Nothing had worms. "It's good," she said.

Her mother looked betrayed, but a minute later she was laughing at something Carlo had said.

That night at bedtime, Jake laid out his sleeping bag on Valentine's bedroom floor, saying that the couch was lumpy and her room the only one with carpet. The carpet was made of sample squares, glued together in a checkered grid, green and red and blue.

"What if I sat up at night with a dream," Jake said, "then cracked my head open on the hard floor out there?"

He acted out the head-cracking, making a head-cracked face, and Valentine watched from her pillow. She had tasted the wine and felt nothing from it, only a kind of warmth.

"Is Angela Ellberg pretty?" she heard herself ask.

"Angie?" he said. "Sure. Why?"

"Is your dad in love with her?"

He thought about it. "I don't think so," he said.

"Are you?" She held her breath.

"No," he said scornfully.

They lay in silence for a while, in the light from the

lamp by her bed, and then he sat up suddenly, propping himself on one arm. His eyes were dark and serious.

"Can I kiss you?" he asked.

It took her a second to respond. It wasn't surprise she felt, just unpreparedness. "Why?"

"Because I want to."

Valentine closed her eyes and the kiss was cool and dry. It pressed against her lips for a long moment, and she saw the blaze of light from the bonfire and wanted to climb down into his arms, and then it was gone. The air in front of her face felt empty and cold. Jake lay back with his hands behind his head and looked at the ceiling. Then he looked at her and nodded, as if to say that was what he had wanted.

SEPTEMBER CAME, and her mother had a new job with the state, and Jake went to live with his mother for the school year. One day walking home from the library, Valentine saw him downtown. He had friends with him, and she felt shy and kept walking, and he didn't seem to notice. She looked down to see if she was wearing her cool jeans. She was, but when she checked in a shop window, she saw herself, not tall and cool but small, in a little girl's pink coat.

At a birthday party that weekend, the other girls asked if she had kissed a boy yet. She felt her face burning and refused to answer, and they squealed with delight.

Carlo started coming around more often, now that he lived alone. He settled his lawsuit against the college, which made him happy because it meant he'd been right, but it didn't give him his job back. One day Valentine found him reading the newspaper in the kitchen when she got home from school, and she felt suddenly bold.

"Are you going to live here?" she asked.

He seemed to think about it before he answered. "If I play my cards right," he said.

"Did you ask my mom?"

"Not really," he said. "Not yet."

That night her mother stayed out late, without calling. Valentine ate a grilled-cheese sandwich with Carlo, who taught her sentences in Italian. *Buona sera, signorina! Come ti chiami? Quanti anni hai?*

"God, I miss my job," he said suddenly. He rubbed his eyes with his hands. "I miss it like I used to miss my wife."

They heard Gwen come through the front door, and Carlo frowned. He stood as she walked into the kitchen.

"Where the fuck have you been?" he asked.

"At dinner," she said, sliding her nice jacket off her arms.

"With?"

"A friend," she said. "From work."

"You left Val alone? You didn't call?"

"I knew you'd be here," she said. "You're *always* here." She went into her bedroom and shut the door.

Carlo looked at Valentine and sighed. "I don't ask for so much," he said. After a while he knocked at the bedroom door and after some discussion went inside.

THE NEXT MORNING was a Saturday. When Valentine got up in her nightgown, there was pancake smell from the kitchen. Her mother stood at the stove, and Carlo sat at the kitchen table, pouring chokecherry syrup on his pancakes.

"The risen Beatrice," he said, pulling out a chair for her. "Whose clear eyes see all."

"Hi, baby," her mother said, but her voice sounded unhappy.

There was a long silence.

"I think we're too cooped up here," Carlo said. "Let's all take a trip and go camping. Jake, too."

"We already have a trip planned," Gwen said.

"Great, where?"

"My parents want to see Val. It's just us."

Carlo scowled at his plate, and knocked over his orange juice so it dripped onto the floor. He jumped up to keep it off his jeans, and Gwen wiped the table in annoyed silence.

They took up the subject of the trip after breakfast, their voices barely muffled by the closed bedroom door. "I went through this with my wife," Carlo was saying. "I won't go through it again."

Valentine climbed up the tree to the roof and crouched at the edge to spin maple seeds to the ground, her toes almost out in the air. The last time she had been on the roof with Jake, talking about their parents, he had said, "They kiss with tongue."

Valentine had been surprised to hear him say it only because it was so obvious—she had seen them do it a million times. But Jake had been living with his mother, who probably didn't do that.

"Gross," Valentine had said, in a tentative way, hoping that was the right response.

Jake said, "I don't think it's gross," but he didn't sound sure. He flicked a maple seed with his finger and thumb, and it sailed out in a long curve, then spun to the ground.

Valentine had eyed him sideways, wondering if he wanted to try it. She wanted to, suddenly: she wanted to know what it was like. And why would he mention it if he didn't? Then the front door had slammed—Gwen and Carlo fighting, like they were now—and Carlo shouted, "Jake!"

"I better go," Jake had said, and he was down the tree and gone.

Now, alone on the roof, Valentine looked at her shoes and wished people would either stay or go away, but not constantly be coming back and leaving again. She guessed by *people* she meant Jake. Her father hadn't come back in a long time.

The door slammed and Carlo passed below her without looking up, got into his car in the driveway, and drove away.

She climbed down and went into the house, where her mother sat cross-legged on the bedroom floor, her face in her hands.

"We're taking a trip?" Valentine asked.

"We are now," her mother said.

It was a long drive in hot weather, and they kept the windows down and listened to tapes. Gwen sang along to Joan Armatrading in a clear, thin voice—*"I'm lucky, I'm lucky, I can walk under ladders . . ."* Valentine watched the trees and fields and telephone poles go by. Her grandparents' house was big and neat and looked over a valley. Her grandfather was tall and silver-haired, and her grandmother was blond, and they walked and spoke briskly. Valentine and her mother shared a room with two single beds, where Gwen sometimes cried without warning. There were sweet pea blossoms from the garden on the night table. They all went for a hike to a clear, cold lake. Then they said good-bye. On the long drive home, Valentine asked if they were going to see Carlo anymore.

"Probably not, baby," her mother said.

Valentine looked out the car window.

"I mean, no," her mother said. "I told him we wouldn't. It's over."

Valentine wasn't sure what to say. She was used to Carlo, by now, and she would miss Jake.

They got back to the house in the middle of the night, and Valentine woke to the familiar maple branches outside the windshield, hanging in the pale light from the alley-way. She pretended to be asleep.

"Come on," her mother said. "I'm too tired to carry you."

So Valentine shouldered her backpack and went in. The first thing she noticed was how hot the house was, shock-ingly hot. She stood in the doorway, feeling the strange heat on her face and in her lungs. The house smelled like hot wood. Her mother rushed to turn off the gas heaters, which were blazing, glowing blue in the dark. The hissing, breathing sound of them stopped.

"I turned off the pilot before we left," she said, looking to Valentine. "You saw me do it."

It sounded like an accusation. Valentine didn't remem-ber. "Can I go outside?" she asked. It was so hot, and she was so tired.

"Leave the door open," her mother said, turning on a light.

Valentine sat on the front step in the cool air, listening to her mother open windows, and waited for her eyes to adjust again to the dark. Her mother let out a cry inside the house. Valentine studied the garden on the other side of the clothesline, and it looked strange in the shadows, though she couldn't say why.

Her mother came outside, and her voice was small and choked. "He was here," she said. "He took things. That necklace he gave me, and some photographs."

Valentine was sorry about the necklace, and wondered which photographs.

"I guess it's better that he lit the pilot," her mother said, getting her own voice back. "But I can't *believe* him."

Valentine was too sleepy to respond, and she didn't really understand about the pilot. She was still looking at the garden, its shapes coming into focus. Her mother looked, too.

"Oh—" Gwen said, ducking under the clothesline. She kneeled in the dirt.

Valentine followed. The neat rows of lettuce had been ripped out, head by head, and left to lie there. The ground was cool and damp from the timed water, and the lettuce was still green, only trampled and wilted. The roots had been kicked up, and the carrots pulled and broken, and the strawberries ground into mush. The raspberry bushes that hung over the garden had been cut so the branches lay with their crushed fruit on the ground. The smell was of wet dirt and sweet berries and green leaves and rot. Valentine sat among the ruined heads of lettuce, and her mother lay down with a little moan and rested her head on Valentine's knee.

Her mother's hair was soft beneath her hand and she thought of Carlo jimmying the door and turning on the heat. She wondered if her father would have done something like that, if he'd stayed in town—if that was why it was impossible for him to stay. She guessed he wouldn't have, but she couldn't be sure. She wondered if Jake had been with Carlo, if he had stomped with his father through the plants, laughing, kicking the lettuce heads like soccer balls.

She thought they might sleep out here in the yard. It was so cool and quiet and dark, and the house was so hot. The thought that she would never see Jake again—not in the same way—made her sadder than the ruined garden or the missing things. She thought of him on her bedroom floor, propped on one arm to kiss her, and how cool and soft it felt, and then how it was gone.

AGUSTÍN

THE LIGHT in the morning made him happy. It was one of the few things that did now. It arrived discreetly filtered, not to disturb him, then poured in when Pablino came to open the shutters, lighting up the dark corners and bleaching the embroidery on the nineteenth-century bench at the foot of the bed.

Agustín didn't care about the embroidery. His daughters did; they said it was fading. The bench had come from an estate auction, at which someone's children sold everything and split the money so they wouldn't fight. His daughters wouldn't have an auction when he died; they loved to fight, and would agree only in condemning his treatment of the furniture. When the generals were taking everything, all the best houses, Agustín had hidden his property behind unpruned trees, let the buildings go to hell, and drained the lake until it became a fetid swamp, something the generals could not want. When the junta was thrown out, and other families opened their houses for dances and dinners, Agustín didn't. He hired gardeners, and the lake filled itself back in, but he stayed alone, behind the trees. But today his daughter was coming to lunch. It was easier to hide from the generals than from those girls.

Alma, his elder daughter, was preoccupied with her spoiled teenage children, but found time to telephone him about nothing. Lucha, the younger, was very thin, and recently blond, and appeared in magazines with fruit on her head, which deeply upset her aunts. She was a singer, of sorts, and childless in her thirties. Agustín sometimes wondered if the girls would be more tolerable if their mother had lived. They had been thirteen and fifteen when she died of a melanoma no one had noticed, and it seemed to have arrested them at that selfish age.

Agustín read the newspaper in bed, finished the orange juice and croissant off the tray, and ate the remaining jam with the coffee spoon. Then he rose to go outside. He wanted to prepare an English lesson for Pablino, or to begin reading a new book that had arrived, about the battle of Trafalgar, but Lucha would interrupt anything he began.

He walked to the stables, where the groom had bandaged the leg of the new quarter horse. Agustín inspected the wrapping, to be sure it was clean, and the horse rubbed its heavy head against his shoulder, smelling of sweat and liniment. At the simplicity of the gesture, he felt a pang: the raw nerve of his loneliness exposed.

Out of loneliness, he had gone to a party in Buenos Aires for the Prince of Wales. He had watched the white-haired women in pearls and their men in dinner jackets, people who had railed against England over the Malvinas, shoving each other out of the way to get close to the prince. A woman had broken her necklace in the rush, and crawled after the pearls on the floor. Another had dug her heel into Agustín's shoe. They were hardy and ruthless, his contemporaries, these people who had survived everything.

It was that night after the party, as Pablino was driving him home on the bad roads, that Agustín had offered to teach the boy English. Pablino was an Indian, small and agile, with pockmarks beneath his high cheekbones. He was also an orphan, his father killed in the miserable war, his mother of an unnamed disease. Asked his age, he answered without confidence: he was twenty-eight or twenty-nine. He seemed both younger and older than his years. He wasn't forthcoming about his past, though Agustín knew he had picked cotton for his grandfather as a boy, and had rarely gone to school. He seemed uninterested in the future, although it was hard for Agustín to know. But he spoke of no plans.

"I must be too old to learn English," he said.

"Nonsense," Agustín said. "You're still a child."

They had begun with simple greetings the next day: good morning, hello, how are you. Pablino seemed politely interested in the lessons, but he gave nothing away, and Agustín thought he might seem politely interested if his employer offered to shoot an apple off his head.

Lucha and her husband arrived for lunch in their spotless gold car on the gravel drive. His skinny daughter climbed out in gold sandals that left her feet almost bare and a buttery pantsuit that swung loose around her ankles. The husband had a gut like all Americans, and wore sunglasses and shorts. He spoke Spanish like a tourist, and made no effort to learn more. Agustín had a grudging respect for the man's stubbornness. They spoke English together.

"I have a new gun to show you," Agustín told him. "An elephant gun."

"Oh, those guns!" Lucha said. She kissed him on the cheek. She was very tan, as if nothing had happened to her mother. "Why don't you ever come to the city, Papi? We miss you so."

He wasn't fooled by her flattery. He had been in an accident in a hired car not long ago, and Lucha hadn't been able to conceal her disappointment that he was still alive, spending her money. He tried to think back to a happier time— two round little girls in his lap, a living, loving wife—but it was no longer he. Children were experiments, and his had failed.

He led his guests to the patio for a drink. Lucha asked Pablino for a Coca-Cola Light and his son-in-law asked for whiskey. Such things, before lunch.

"I wish you hadn't rented the summer house to the French lady," his daughter began.

"She's a good tenant."

"People take their lovers there, and pretend they don't have wives and husbands somewhere else."

"Oh, Lucha," he said. "What else is new?"

"They swim naked in the pool."

"And?"

"And it's embarrassing! Our caretakers are there."

"Adulterers tip well."

"Papi, don't you care about *anything*? If Mami were alive, she would care."

If Mami were alive. That was always the thing. "They are old bodies in an old pool," he said. "What does it matter?"

Lucha slumped back, pouting. "Well," she said. "You won't believe who came to me for a job. Inez Martín."

Agustín caught his breath at the rush of feeling in his chest. He shifted in his chair, trying to understand this news.

"Do you remember the Martíns?" Lucha asked. "They went away after Menem came. They lost everything."

"I thought she was in Italy."

"She came back," Lucha said. "She's been working here. I needed a second housekeeper, and Ofelia let her in. I couldn't believe it. I used to idolize her. She was older than I was, and so glamorous, in beautiful clothes. And there she was on my sofa, in a cotton dress and cheap shoes. She wasn't surprised to see me, she knew who the job was for."

Agustín waited for the rest of the story. The little black dog came to the table, the one the maid spoiled and the cook overfed, and Lucha began to rub its head. She made small kissing noises over the arm of her chair, and the dog wriggled with happiness.

"Her husband?" Agustín finally asked.

"He had a heart attack, I think," she said. "But he didn't die."

Agustín tried to remain composed. Inez Martín! She had utterly disrupted his life. They had met in the house of a friend, and she had talked very charmingly at dinner, and touched his arm in a way that gave him encouragement. It was a hundred years ago: twenty years ago, at least. She was much younger than he. He had persuaded her to meet him in the garden. Her dreadful husband was asleep in the house. Agustín's wife was dead, and Inez brought him back to the world. He remembered her warm breath and the taste of her, and the cold stone bench beneath them. He thought he had been saved. He had pursued her through other people's houses, meeting in empty rooms when the others were out. The chance of catching her eye and slipping away was what he lived for. He was exultant in the conquest. Then the inconvenient husband lost his position and his money, and Inez went with him to Italy, where he had family, to start again. The husband was a bore; not even failure could make him interesting. Agustín had begged her to stay but she left, and he had heard nothing since.

"I couldn't hire her, of course," Lucha said. "She's my equal. I couldn't have her washing my underwear. So I sent her to the crazy French, who wouldn't know anything or care. Poor Inez."

"She's at the summer house?"

"I think so," Lucha said. "Imagine, with the naked guests!"

There was a long silence. The little dog yipped, at being ignored, and Lucha reached down to take its ears in both hands. "What *is* it?" she asked, as the dog panted with pleasure. "What is *wrong*, my love?"

"How about seeing that elephant gun?" the American husband asked.

"Such a waste of money," Lucha said.

"It's an investment," Agustín said, out of habit. "And I'm going to Africa."

Lucha looked up at him with her mother's big eyes. *"What?"* she asked.

The plan hadn't existed until that moment. He had killed a rhinoceros and a bear many years ago, and mounted them on the walls, but he was old now. Even the rhinoceros and the bear were shot under circumstances in which it was not difficult to shoot a large animal. He had bought the elephant gun because it was a magnificent firearm for his collection. But now he thought Africa might do him good.

"I'm going to kill an elephant," he said. He knew there was an English story about the embarrassment of doing so, but he couldn't remember it clearly. Why should he not shoot an elephant?

The three of them went to his office, where Pablino unlocked the glass case containing the best guns.

Lucha perched on the edge of the desk. "You're so lucky to have Pablino," she said in English. "Ofelia is hopeless. Inez at least would be smart. Someday I'm going to steal Pablino from you." She gave the boy a big, seductive smile.

Pablino passed the gun to Agustín, ignoring her. The boy might not understand her English, but he understood Lucha well enough. The gun was heavy, a double-barreled rifle that could put a bullet through an elephant's skull. Agustín handed it to the American, who let out a low whistle.

"That's gotta have some kick," he said.

"I suppose so."

"Let's go see!" Lucha said, springing up off the desk.

Agustín had not thought of shooting the gun—the car-

tridges were expensive and the recoil was intimidating—
but he felt himself pushed along by the children. Lucha had
an idea where to go, and they all climbed into Agustín's
little Renault, Lucha driving and Agustín in the passenger
seat with the gun. The American folded his big legs into
the back. They drove through the pastures, past the cows,
and Agustín got out to open and close each gate. The sky
was expansive and blue, and he found his own property
majestic. He thought of Inez, who had never seen it—it
was still an overgrown swamp when he was chasing her
around other people's houses, keeping her a secret from his
tyannical teenage daughters. But she couldn't fail to find it
majestic, too.

"Here," Lucha said finally, and she parked the Renault
at the end of a road, by the lake that had been drained
and now was full again. "We used to come here when we
were little." She walked, looking up at the trees, her trou-
ser legs swinging around her ankles. "There," she said, and
she pointed. Above them, hanging like a giant wasps' nest
from a high branch, was a brown woven bulb: a nest of
papagayos.

"I'm not going to shoot parrots with an elephant gun,"
Agustín said.

"You should see if it works, before you go off to Africa."
She was daring him, taunting.

"I want to go back to the house."

"Just try to hit *something*," Lucha said. She picked up

a fallen branch with leaves still on it. "We'll put this on top of the fencepost, and you can shoot it off." She balanced it carefully across the post, brushed off her hands, and stepped back.

Agustín studied the branch on the fence, not twenty feet away. If this branch were the only kind of target he could hit, they would have to hold the elephant on a leash for him. He loaded the rifle, thinking he might as well burn money, then raised it and fired. The kick was much greater than he expected, and he stumbled backward. The shot missed the fencepost, but broke a piece of barbed wire that waved in the air. The parrots fled the nest overhead, screeching. He thought he might have dislocated his shoulder, the pain was so intense. He investigated the mobility of his arm. The branch sat untouched, and the screaming of the birds faded into silence.

"You should be careful," Lucha said mildly, "that the elephant doesn't get angry and come after you."

"You want me to die anyway."

"Of course I don't!"

"I want to go back to the house." His shoulder was bruised and his hands trembled. He got in the car with the muzzle of the gun between his feet, and let the American open the first gate.

Riding past the field of alfalfa growing for winter hay, Agustín saw a hare out the window, darting along the road just ahead of them, and he knew he could shoot it. He would be ready for the kick now. He roared at Lucha to stop the car and lifted the gun, keeping an eye on the hare. Then the car was filled with the loudest noise he had ever heard, as loud as a bomb, and the car shuddered as Lucha braked to a stop. A sharp smell of powder hung in the air. He looked down at the floor between his feet. A ragged circle the size of a dessert plate had been blasted away, and he could see the gravel of the road below. He seemed to have hit nothing important: the engine still chugged.

Lucha swore loudly and shrilly. "What if that had been my *head*?" she cried.

It could more likely have been Agustín's own foot. The gun had nearly jumped out of his hands. He didn't look at Lucha, or at her husband in the back seat. There would have been nothing left of the hare, in the unlikely event he had hit it. He put the safety on, although the gun was now empty. Lucha stomped on the gas, and the car lurched forward. Agustín watched the hole in the floor, the road moving in streaks of gray and brown below. He was ashamed, but he wouldn't give his daughter any quarter.

They drove along the windbreak of trees, past the lawn and up to the house. Pablino came out to meet them, looked alarmed, and helped Agustín with something like tenderness into the house.

The three of them sat over an awkward lunch, Pablino bringing the plates and taking them away. The boy moved quietly and missed nothing. As the husband reached for a dropped fork, Pablino appeared with a new one on a plate. Agustín kept feeling the kick of the gun, and a ringing in his ears.

"Tell me more about the girl," he said, when the dessert finally came. "Inez Martín."

"She's not a girl anymore," Lucha said. "She's older than I am."

"How old?"

"Oh, God, maybe forty-five? She's not young."

It was hard to imagine. In his mind, Inez was in her twenties, a young wife, and he was trying to steal her away. At first she said she couldn't leave her husband because she stood to lose everything. Later she couldn't leave him because he had lost so much. And now she was working as a maid for a capricious Frenchwoman. Life could punch you in the throat no matter how you chose.

His daughter's husband stretched his arms, presenting his belly and big chest. "Want to go to the yacht club Saturday and look at boats?" he asked. "There's a race, so they'll have some good ones."

"I have to get the car fixed," Agustín said. "And make plans for Africa."

"Oh, Papi!" Lucha said. "*Africa*. You almost shot my head off!"

She gave Agustín a perfunctory kiss as they left. She smelled of flowers. He wondered how Inez smelled: of washing powder, or the kitchen, or some perfume from her life before. Lucha lifted her gold sandals into her husband's car, and they drove away.

T HE FRENCHWOMAN met Agustín at the door of his mother's summer house herself, not sending someone to do it. Her hair was chestnut brown and her face was stretched smooth, but he wasn't fooled. She was as old as he. She wore a long green silk robe with an embroidered neckline, and her arms were tan. He had called to say he would like to speak to Inez.

"It's wonderful to see you," the Frenchwoman said. "I've been so happy in your house."

He murmured some approving sounds.

"Inez is a good maid," she said. "Are you looking for someone to work? I can't spare her right away, but eventually I can, when I go to France. I can take with me only the ones I brought."

"Of course."

"There's a sitting room there," the Frenchwoman said. "You know the house, of course. Will you stay for lunch?"

"No, thank you," he said. "I'm engaged for lunch."

She shrugged in a French way, disbelieving him, still smiling. "I'll send her in."

The room was painted red. His mother had read to him there before dinner, when he was a child: a thrilling half hour of warmth and comfort, under a throw blanket, enveloped in his mother's perfume, with the dogs sitting at their feet. The walls had been pale yellow. There was a television in the corner now, and a wheeled liquor cart. He was still absorbing the changes when Inez Martín appeared in a pink maid's dress and a white apron. She wore her dark hair pulled back, and sat on the edge of a leather chair with her hands on her narrow knees. There were lines around the dark eyes he had loved, and the skin over her temples seemed very thin and pale, with a blue vein visible on one side, but she had the same pointed chin, the same clever mouth. His heart was racing. He hadn't expected to have all the old feelings in their full strength. He had thought they would be diminished by time.

"I thought you were in Italy," he said cautiously.

"I came back."

"And your husband? His heart?"

"He's recovering."

He nodded. She had a small, dark, triangular scar on her smooth bare shin. Her wedding band seemed loose on her finger. She had a slight accent, from the years in Italy. He tried to clear his mind. "You saw my daughter Lucha," he said.

"I did."

"She's not my finest achievement."

Inez laughed. He remembered her laugh. It had charmed him that first night at dinner. "It was perverse to go to the interview," she said. "I was trying to destroy my pride, so it couldn't torment me anymore. The way they cauterize a wound. It didn't work. But it did get me a job, finally."

"It's very good to see you."

"I don't know if it's good to see you. My old decadent life." She rested her elbow on the arm of the chair. "What news do you bring me? Is it as glamorous as I remember, or as sordid as it is here?"

"It isn't very glamorous."

"It's the most ugly thing you can imagine, here," she said. "People with everything, who take everything for granted."

"I'm sorry to hear that."

"Some are your friends."

"Once they were," he said. "I'm very much alone, these days."

She looked thoughtful. "Do you know what I miss?" she asked. "I miss orange juice in the morning, in bed. I miss someone bringing in a tray, and opening the windows."

Agustín felt an aching thrill at how easy this would be to supply.

"It's foolish, isn't it?" she asked.

Agustín said he didn't think it foolish at all. His heart felt dangerously full, for the first time in years. That dried-up, battered organ, suddenly flush with love. It could kill him.

"It *is* foolish, though," she said. "The money is gone, and my husband thinks of nothing else. My son is in boarding school, so all the money goes there, and to the doctors."

He was trying to keep up. "You have a son?"

"Of course." She smiled and looked much younger, the way he remembered her. "He's thirteen," she said. "The age when they become awkward and skinny, but he is still so beautiful. The most beautiful child. All I want is for him not to be ashamed of me."

He wished he had known about the son. He had deliberately avoided gossip, but how had word of a child not reached him? Why had Lucha not told him?

"I want you to marry me," he blurted. He hadn't intended to say it outright, but it seemed best to be direct, as she was. He had to lay his cards on the table.

There was a pause. "I'm married," she said, without surprise or resentment.

"But are you happy? Does he treat you well?"

She studied his face. "You want to spite your daughters."

"No." He shook his head. He wanted to kiss her again in a dark garden, but the dream was complicated by the vision of a lanky adolescent sitting beside her in the shadows, glowering. "I could help your son," he said. "I could pay for the school."

"You weren't counting on a child when you came here."

"No."

"But you're serious."

"I always was." It wasn't entirely true. He had been too afraid of his teenage daughters to offer her marriage, then. He had been a fool.

She took another moment, as if thinking it through. "A déclassée housemaid leaving her child and sick husband for money," she said. "Imagine. Your servants would hate me, and your daughters would hate me, and my son would certainly hate me. I'm strong enough for this kind of work, but I'm not strong enough to be alone and hated."

Agustín wanted to say that she wouldn't be alone, but he understood that she didn't agree. "Where will you go when the Frenchwoman leaves?" he asked, through the haze of shame and disappointment.

"I'll find another job."

"You're not young." They were Lucha's words only, called up by his misery, because Inez did seem young to him.

She paused, and then she said, "No, I'm not. Is that what you came to tell me?"

He reproached himself for offending her. "I only meant that the work must be difficult," he said. "You should have some relief."

"I know exactly how difficult my work is."

"I could help your son," he said. "Anonymously, for nothing. School fees, books, whatever he needs. Holidays. I would like to do that."

She laughed for a second time. "Lucha would love that."

"It isn't her money."

She considered him for a long moment. "It's tempting," she said. "But no, I think temptation is a dangerous thing. We have what we need. It's kind of you to offer."

"Please." He could hear the panic in his voice, at the thought of going home alone. He had refused to think that far ahead, to anticipate defeat, but now it loomed: the despair of the drive back, the months and years. "For your son," he said.

"It was kind of you to visit," she said. "I should help with the lunch." She rose, the woman he had wanted so desperately, and she smoothed the skirt of the pink maid's dress before she went out.

A T THE FRONT DOOR, the comically smooth-faced Frenchwoman touched his arm. She said, in a confidential tone, that Inez could act a bit *de haut*, but she was honest and did good work. If he wanted her sooner, that could be arranged. He should only let her know. Agustín could hardly reply, and couldn't hide his unhappiness. Pablino opened the car door for him, with what seemed like an extra degree of care, and Agustín tried to control his trembling hands. If he held them tightly together, his hands were still, but then they were useless. The Frenchwoman watched them drive away. The little Renault had been deemed drivable, with a flat piece of wood covering the hole in the floor. He was going home to eat his lunch alone. He could go to Africa after all. He could let someone lead him to an infirm elephant and he could shoot it until it fell down. Pablino drove the damaged car carefully onto the main road. It occurred to Agustín that the Frenchwoman's servants would have given Pablino a coffee while he waited, and the boy would have heard the gossip of the house.

"What do they say in the kitchen about the maid Inez?" he asked.

Pablino hesitated, and said nothing.

"You can tell me," he said.

"That she is beautiful."

"What else?"

"That she was rich once."

"They don't accept her."

"No."

Agustín nodded. So Inez was alone and hated already. She was living this way for her son, for whom she would do anything. He tried to imagine working as a servant in order not to make his daughters ashamed. It was ridiculous; the very act would shame them. There was a small, ugly part of him that wished for her son to recoil from her, because she had chosen servitude over Agustín's offer. But her son would love her, as he did. The boy made everything worthwhile for her. His existence made her grateful that Agustín had been too cowardly to defy his daughters for love.

"Is there anything this afternoon?" he asked Pablino.

"Nothing," Pablino said.

"Thank you for driving me."

Pablino glanced at him in surprise. It was his job. It was uncomfortable, Pablino's clear understanding that something significant had happened.

"I'm grateful," Agustín said clumsily. "You drive well."

The wounded car rattled along. He would go home and have his lunch, and Pablino would clear it away. They could have an English lesson; the boy would conjugate verbs if asked. There was the book on Trafalgar to begin. His older daughter would call to complain and brag about her children, to remind him that they existed, his heirs. Lucha would call to ask if the car was fixed and if he was really going to Africa.

He remembered the enormous sound of the gun going off, and felt the kick again. A purplish bruise had developed on his shoulder. If Lucha had never come to lunch, he wouldn't have made a fool of himself in so many ways. He would never have fired the gun, or shot out the floor. He wouldn't have known that Inez Martín had resurfaced in his mother's house, and he wouldn't have presented himself to the vain, silly Frenchwoman, or prostrated himself before Inez. He would be living his muted and uneventful life, unbruised, with his books and his horses and his house. If the trees could protect him from the pain that now gnawed at his heart, he would let them grow huge, but the trees could do nothing. He wanted to weep, but Pablino would be mortified, so he checked himself. He held his hands tightly together and cursed his daughter for bringing the terrible world, with its humiliation and longing, back to his door.

THE CHILDREN

FIELDING ARRIVED at the lake house ahead of his wife, to find a rusted Volvo station wagon parked in the driveway. He knew the car, knew the cracked, sun-bleached upholstery and the embroidered Chinese good luck charm hanging from the rearview mirror. His wife would be out after work, to meet him for dinner, but her car wasn't there. It was summer, the sun still bright on the water, and no lights were on in the house. Fielding watched the blank windows, waiting for a clue, and then he carried the groceries inside.

Jennie Taylor sat at the kitchen table with her legs

crossed, in jeans and a sweater. Her dark hair was brushed straight and smooth. Fresh air and her mother's looks had served her well. The boxy station wagon had been her parents' car before it was hers, and Fielding was amazed it still ran.

"I let myself in," she said.

"Good." He set the paper grocery bag on the counter and thought that nothing needed to go in the fridge. Jennie had spent so much time at the house that she knew where the key was hidden. It was the second time he had been alone with her in there, and the first time still filled him with regret. She had been staying with his family, flirting with him all weekend, and it had caught him off guard. She wasn't the pigtailed child of his friends anymore; she had come back from college transformed, a self-assured young woman, sunning herself in a bikini on the deck. At the end of the weekend, she had stayed behind while he locked up—he wasn't trying to diminish his own part in the thing, but she had stayed behind—and she had stepped into his arms, so agreeably sun-warm and strong. He had kissed her at some length before stopping. It paled now, as a transgression, but at the time he had suffered the tortures of the damned.

"You're meeting Meg?" he asked. It was a bluff; he knew his daughter was staying in town. His son, Gavin, had been vague, as usual.

"No," Jennie said.

"My wife will be out, too."

"I guessed," she said.

"Is anyone else coming?"

Jennie shrugged.

He turned on a kitchen light, in case the others arrived, but the pale bulb was overwhelmed by the slanting sunlight. He opened the pantry closet and started the hot water heater. He wondered how many more times he would do that, and what would happen to the lake house—a winterized shack when they bought it, now a maze of additions—once he got up the nerve to tell his wife. She was a lawyer and would have the upper hand.

"You're leaving Raye," Jennie said.

He felt a surge of adrenaline, and steadied himself on the closet door. "Does it show?" he asked.

Jennie smiled. "I've known you since I was born," she said. "You think that means you know me inside out, but really it means I know you."

He thought of correcting her: he had known her *before* she was born. He'd watched her mother, hugely pregnant and happy, floating in the lake with her belly at the surface. Her father so proud you'd think no one had ever knocked up a pretty girl before. The two families had done everything together, before Jennie's began to disintegrate. Jennie was his daughter's age, two years younger than his son, and he remembered her at six in just a bikini bottom, darting in and out of the water. Or bundled in a snowsuit in winter, riding a plastic sled on her stomach across the ice. She was twelve when the marriage finally ended, and her father had sung drunkenly, here in the lake-house kitchen, *"If you want to be happy for the rest of your life, don't make a pret-ty woman your wife,"* and then cried over what the divorce might do to Jennie.

"Does my family know I'm leaving?" he asked her now.

"I don't think so," she said. "It was my mother who saw you. In a car, with a girl. She asked me if she should tell Raye. I told her not to."

"Thank you," he said.

"My mom kept telling me it was my swimming teacher. That really upset her."

"She hasn't been that for years."

"Is that what you tell yourself?" she asked. "Does it help?"

"I'm not doing this lightly," he said.

He knew what he was getting into. He had thought of taking his mistress away from the town he'd lived in all his life, rather than face the collective disapproval. Eleanor had taught everyone's kids to swim; she had a gift for it, even as a teenager. They had all watched from the park benches outside the chain-link fence at the pool, while Eleanor coaxed their children to swim toward her, to reach and pull, breathe and blow. The chlorine gave her hair an angelic sparkle, and she had lovely breasts in her red swimsuit; she exuded encouragement and warmth. Now she had moved home, and those parents who had watched were going to judge him, when he had known them all in the wild old days, getting high while the kids slept on the floor, wandering off with someone else's wife.

"You think Eleanor's a strange choice," he said.

"Were you sleeping with her back then?"

"Of course not."

"Why 'of course not'?" she asked. "Why wouldn't I wonder?"

"Because she was a child. She was seventeen."

Jennie rolled her eyes.

"I saw her in the hardware store a few months ago," he said. "She was buying a nightlight. I hadn't thought about her for years, I had forgotten her name."

"Do you know how you'll break it to Raye?"

"I haven't gotten that far."

"She'll freak."

"She's very resourceful," he said. It was true. You could drop his wife alone in the dark woods and she would make tools out of nothing, build herself a shelter and tame the bears.

"Does she know about us?" Jennie asked.

He wanted to say that there wasn't much to know, but he said, "No. She wouldn't let ammunition like that lie around."

"Did you ever tell my dad?"

"Of course not."

"You haven't seen him lately."

Fielding thought of the fat joints smoked on the deck,

and Frank Taylor holding forth over a glass of scotch, a million years ago. The children played an elaborate game of tag, using the dock and the beach and the little rowboat. Gavin galloped along behind Meg and Jennie; the girls were younger but imperious and in control. Their hair was like the dry grass on the hillside, their bare feet toughened by summer. They moved as effortlessly into the boat and across the water—pulling one oar hard, spinning the boat around the dock—as across the land. Amphibious children. "We're creating little hedonists," Frank used to say. "Nothing will be as pleasurable as this for the rest of their lives. They'll search everywhere for something that can measure up, and nothing will."

"You're going to hear from him, when he finds out you're leaving," Jennie said now. "He thinks divorce ruined his life."

"Did it?"

"Sure," Jennie said. "I mean, it ruined what *was* his life." She studied him. "Why are you doing this?"

"Because I can't imagine doing anything else."

"I feel like kind of an expert," she said, "because I've thought about how long sex with someone younger could keep you interested, and how soon you'd be tired of it. And what it would do to you to horrify everyone you know, and be stranded with someone who's basically a kid. Who's going to want kids of her own. You know Eleanor will want kids, right?"

"I'm not sure."

"I used to have this fantasy," she said. "It's so stupid. I can tell you now. You would leave Raye for me, and it would be a huge scandal, but we would go to my dad together and explain it. It would be a shock to him, but he would get over it, and you would be friends again. It's a crazy fantasy, but I wanted it."

Fielding heard a car pull up outside.

"But I *never* would have asked you to do it," she whispered earnestly. "I'm not insane. And then my mother saw you in that car. God. Gavin's here."

The screen door slammed shut and his son was in the room, in the baseball cap and sweatpants he wore to coach soccer. Fielding was struck by how much his son looked like him: the broad face, the comic slant of the eyebrows. Lately, his children's adult presence made him feel very old.

"Hey!" Gavin said, with undisguised joy at seeing Jennie, and Fielding understood that his son was in love, unrequited. She took the tribute seated, like a queen.

"Are Mom and Meg coming?" Gavin asked. "This'll be great."

Fielding looked at Jennie, and she at him. He knew the correct thing was to be casual with his son, to act natural, but he couldn't seem to do the correct thing anymore. He was afraid of the look in Jennie's eye, and of what she might say. She might tell Gavin that his father had taken up with their childhood swimming teacher, and his mother would be on her own. He prepared himself for the girl to say it, and perversely hoped she would. He would have to say it soon if she didn't.

"Is everything okay?" Gavin asked. He went to the pantry closet. "Hot water's on," he announced.

Jennie shook her head almost imperceptibly at Fielding, but he didn't know what she meant. *Don't say anything? I won't say anything? You're in for it now?*

Gavin was frowning at them, scowling the way he had as a child when the headaches came on, before they got him glasses. He always said the scowling helped diminish the headaches. It was like limping, he said, to scrunch up his face. It occurred to Fielding that Jennie might see the appeal in Gavin's fresh, untapped devotion. She would tell his son her secrets, lying in bed, her smooth knee thrown over his strong legs. Kissing his father would be only one of them. She was so young and untroubled by guilt, she could tell everything and be forgiven.

Another engine stopped outside, and a car door closed decisively. His wife, arriving for dinner. She would find the children there, but that could be normal, unremarkable.

Raye came into the house in a long, waistless dress, her angular body suggested within it. Her shoulders were freckled, her hair thick and brown with defiant gray streaks, and she carried a bottle of wine. She smiled at Jennie with as much friendliness and warmth as a woman who has been beautiful can muster, when surprised by a girl half her age.

"Jennie, honey," she said. "And Gavin. I didn't know it was a party."

No one said anything, and Raye's face clouded with puzzlement.

"Why are you all looking at me like that?" She looked from Jennie to Gavin. "Oh, shit," she said. "Are you two—"

Jennie shook her head. "No."

Gavin seemed to blush.

"Oh, thank God," Raye said, laughing with relief. "I thought you were going to tell me you were pregnant or something. I was going to need more than a glass of wine for that." She smiled at them all, waiting to be told what was really going on.

Still no one said anything. Fielding thought he had lost the power of speech.

"I'll open this," Raye said, brandishing her wine bottle.

"You're sleeping with Jennie," Gavin said with horror.

"No," Fielding said.

"*What?*" Raye asked.

"Then why are you acting this way?" his son asked.

"I'm not acting any way."

"Why is Jennie here?" Gavin asked.

Fielding tried to think what to say. He wasn't ready to tell them about Eleanor. He cast around for a way to explain.

"I came looking for you," Jennie said to Gavin.

"For me?" He was flattered.

"But your dad was here, so we started talking about my dad."

"Your poor dad," Raye said. "How's he doing?"

Fielding watched them draw closer to Jennie, all suspicion gone, and he marveled. She was a born adulterer.

"I think about him all the time," Raye said, sinking into one of the kitchen chairs. "After the divorce, your mom seemed to need us more, and we kind of lost track."

"He wasn't easy to be with," Jennie said.

Raye shook her head, wanting to be reassured, but not wanting to let go of her own interesting guilt. Fielding found a corkscrew and opened the bottle of wine. He poured some for Jennie, for Raye, and for his son. They ignored him as irrelevant, a waiter filling glasses. He wanted to dance with relief that the situation in the kitchen had stabilized, but instead he washed the lettuce, and salted and peppered the steaks.

"I'll start the grill," Gavin said.

"I should go," Jennie said.

"No!" Gavin pleaded.

"Oh, please stay for dinner," Raye said. "Tell her to stay, honey."

Fielding held his hands up, helplessly.

"My dad's expecting me," Jennie said. "I have to go."

She hugged Raye and Gavin goodbye. Then, in a perfectly natural way, she hugged Fielding, letting her breasts press against him. "I'll tell my dad you said hi," she said.

If he had been smooth, like she was, Fielding would have had an answer that meant one thing to Jennie and another to Raye and Gavin. Instead he said, "Thank you," as if something were caught in his throat. He coughed.

With Jennie gone, they settled into the reflexive movements of a family dinner: Raye set the table, Gavin took the steaks out to the grill, Fielding tossed the salad. All the while he felt a buzzing anxiety in his chest and ears, a heightened awareness and a dread of what might come next. It was possible that nothing would. He could take Jennie's advice, and find a way to let Eleanor go. Jennie could convince her mother that she had seen nothing important in that car, if anyone could. Fielding could stay with his wife, who now passed him the bread bowl and poured him more wine.

They had twice in their marriage seen counselors, a practice Fielding found ridiculous, but he had thought lately about what the professionals might say. They would tell him to stay, because they were marriage counselors, conservative by nature, interested in preserving whatever stability people had patched together. In his mind, there was no argument he could make that would convince them he was doing the right thing. He cut into his steak, which was nicely pink at the center, rich and brown on the outside; he had taught Gavin well. His children had faith in marriage as a safe destination, and if he didn't leave, they could go forth into love with their confidence intact.

But Eleanor. The sweetness of lying against her bare shoulder, the softness of everything about her. She was so pliable and willing, vulnerable where his wife was girded and bulletproof. That day in the hardware store, Eleanor was buying a nightlight with a motion detector and he had asked her why. She said she woke up at night.

"Are you worried?" he asked.

"Oh, sometimes," she said.

"What do you do when you wake up?" He thought she would look as she did now: no makeup, her fine silky hair more mussed. He had wondered if she wore a nightgown.

"I lie awake thinking," she said.

"About what?"

"Oh—everything."

He had liked that *Oh,* the hesitation before the answer. It might be just a tic she had picked up, but it sounded thoughtful.

"Did you always worry?" he asked. "You seemed very cheery in the pool."

"Oh, that pool," she said, exasperated. "That's how every-one thinks of me. I was seventeen, I knew nothing."

"You seem very calm now."

"It makes me less afraid, to act like I'm not."

"What are you afraid of?"

"So many things. Aren't you afraid?"

"Sometimes," he said.

"Yellowstone Park is a giant volcano," she said. "It could explode any day."

"The whole thing?"

"All of it. It would destroy all of the western states and the whole Midwest."

He laughed, at the absurdity of the danger and the earnest look on her face. She had fine blond down near her ears, and freckles across her nose. He wanted to scoop her up in his arms and protect her. "Why tell me that?" he asked. "What good does it do me? When I wake up at night, I'm going to call you and complain. What else do you worry about?"

She smiled. "The usual things. The war, the climate. Flesh-eating bacteria. My parents' health. I think about dumb things, too, stupid things I said. I'll probably regret telling *you* all this. I barely remember your kids. Gavin and Meg, you said?"

The second time they met, in a truck-stop coffee shop beyond the east end of town, where neither of them would know anyone, she ducked her head in embarrassment as she sat down to the table. He told her how bold and brave she was to come.

"I'm not," she said, shaking her head.

"But you're here," he said. "Do you wish you weren't?"

She shook her head again: no.

When her embarrassment seemed to have reached a peak, with the waitress coming by and the big glass door opening every few minutes, when she was practically vibrating with nervousness, he said that he had a house at the lake that was empty and quiet, and they could go have a drink there. They went, and once they were alone, all her anxiety was gone. He had been so happy, with her lying naked and safe in his arms. All he wanted was to preserve that feeling, of the two of them alone together, and make all obstacles to it go away.

Raye was clearing the table now, and Gavin was washing the dishes. Meg had called, late, to check in. When his daughter said, "I love you," before hanging up, Fielding felt a squeeze in his chest. Eleanor was going to want children, in spite of her fears. She was thirty-two, the age for the wanting. Fielding hadn't really absorbed the idea until now. Jennie was right that he hadn't thought it all through. The diapers, the sleeplessness, the willful tyrant two-year-olds, the teacher conferences and dance classes and soccer games. Gavin could teach them soccer moves, but would he want to? Even when Fielding had imagined his grown children being furious with him, he had not imagined it lasting very long, or including new children who would know that their older half-siblings resented their existence. He thought Gavin and Meg were more forgiving than that, but he couldn't be sure. They had never been tested.

Gavin squeezed his father's shoulder and announced he was going back to town. To look for Jennie? He was out the door. Raye took a blanket off the couch and said, "Are you coming outside? It's so nice out."

Fielding went, wondering what he might say to his wife, feeling that he was walking onto a stage without his lines. So there they were on the deck, on the old cushioned chaises longues they had bought together when they were young and too broke to be buying deck furniture. The stars were very clear. A bat flitted by overhead, chasing insects. Raye gave him half the blanket and he pulled it up to his chest, thinking about the nights they had lain like this in college, when he had pretended to look at the stars for a minute or two before diving to get into her pants. Defiant Raye in college, saving the world, going braless with her A-cups; if he went back in time, he couldn't have resisted it.

"Do you think Jennie has a crush on Gavin?" she asked him now. "She said she came looking for him."

"I was thinking that Gavin might have one on her."

"*Really?*" she asked.

"Jennie's an attractive girl," he said. "And she's smart."

"They're like siblings," Raye said. "It would be very strange. He needs someone with a real spark."

He had nothing to gain by extolling Jennie's charms, so he didn't. Raye turned on her side on the deck chair, her body curving toward him under the blanket.

"Do you know who I saw this afternoon?" she asked.

"Do you remember Eleanor Lansing, who taught swimming lessons at the city pool?"

His heart froze. "Eleanor Lansing," he repeated.

"Sturdy blond girl?" she said. "All the dads were in love with her, outside the fence. I bet you were, too, you've just forgotten. She's moved back here to live, to be near her parents."

"Hunh," he said, his mind stumbling over the facts. Why hadn't Eleanor called him the second she escaped the conversation? He wondered if seeing Raye in person had been too much reality, if it had made her rethink stealing Raye's husband. Or if she had only been waiting for him to hear about it. He wanted to jump up from the deck chair and call her now; it was agony to be still.

"*She* had a spark," Raye said, musingly. "I mean, she's too old for Gavin, of course. She had great tits, my God."

"She doesn't anymore?" he asked. Almost anything he said might be held against him later on: anything that suggested that he hadn't seen Eleanor could be construed as an outright lie. He had not expected to be talking about her tits.

"No, I guess she still does," she said. "I just think of her as a teenager in a swimsuit. Like I still think of myself as fifteen years younger. I see myself in the mirror and I think, *Who is that, how did I get so old?* Don't you do that?"

"Of course." They had had this conversation before, and

he had a pang of remorse about jumping ship on her in middle age, trying to swim to a younger boat.

"Eleanor's parents were Republicans or something," she said. "We didn't know them."

He could have told her they were only Lutherans, but didn't. They might as well be Republicans.

"It's funny she's moved back," Raye said. "If Gavin and Meg go away and wait fifteen years to move back, we'll be *really* old."

"They should do what they want."

"But wouldn't it be nice to have them stay?"

"Only if they're happy here."

"Ugh," Raye said. "You should be more selfish, like I am."

Fielding said nothing. Raye reached toward him, under the blanket. He was wearing thick corduroys, and she slipped her hand into his pocket, the thin cotton like a sock on her hand. He felt the usual stirrings, undiminished by the events of the day. He had imagined, very clearly, that he might leave his wife for Eleanor. But could he fuck his wife within minutes of pretending not to know Eleanor, and *then* leave her? He didn't think he could. So could he tell Raye now? He had an opportunity; in a way, she had brought the subject up. But he would have to start talking, right now, and he couldn't begin. So could he *not* fuck his wife, in order not to add insult to injury? She knew just what pressure to use, and now she loosened his belt and slipped her cool hand against his skin.

He opened his eyes and she smiled conspiratorially, and in the dark she looked briefly like the Raye of thirty years ago: the lanky, tender college girl, the wanton defender of the poor. Could he stay and be happy here? Three minutes ago he had been desperate to call Eleanor, to dissect her conversation with his wife, but now he had settled back into the habit of his marriage, of talking in the dark about the children, of his wife's expert hands. He tried to determine if he was paralyzed with indecision or only mired in comfort. He tried to reconstruct his reasons for wanting to leave, but it was like trying, while heavy with sleep in a warm bed, to construct reasons for getting up into the cold.

"You there?" Raye said.

"Yes."

She moved her hand up to his chest, her palm flat beneath his shirt. "What is it you're thinking about doing?" she asked.

"What do you mean?"

"I'm not sure, that's why I'm asking," she said. "I keep feeling that you're half somewhere else, like you're about to bolt."

"Really?"

"Your heart's going crazy, since I asked," she said. "I can feel it."

He tried consciously to slow it down.

"I don't know what's happened," she said. "And I don't want to be a fool here. But for what it's worth, I don't want you to go."

Another bat shot by, a swift black shadow overhead. Fielding's throat felt constricted. He was, even after so much planning, unprepared to speak.

"Babe?" she said.

"I'm not going anywhere." It was the only thing he could say that wouldn't change everything, and he didn't know if he was buying time or if it was true.

"You aren't?" she asked.

He hesitated. "I'm not."

She watched him, his eminently intelligent wife. He pulled her closer to make the scrutiny stop, and feeling her head on his shoulder was reassuring. He was doomed to ambivalence and desire. A braver man, or a more cowardly one, would simply flee. A happier or more complacent man would stay and revel in the familiar, wrap it around him like an old bathrobe. He seemed to be none of those things, and could only deceive the people he loved, and then disappoint and worry them when they saw through him. There was a poem Meg had brought home from college, with the line "Both ways is the only way I want it." The force with which he wanted it both ways made him grit his teeth. What kind of fool wanted it only one way?

It had started to grow cold, on the deck. The stars were

impossibly clear. The bats were out in force. He held his wife and felt himself anchored to everything that was safe and sure, and kept for himself the knowledge of how quickly he could let go and drift free.

O TANNENBAUM

I T WAS A FINE TREE, Everett's daughter agreed. His wife said it was lopsided and looked like a bush. But that was part of its fineness—it was a tall, lopsided Douglas fir, bare on one side where it had crowded out its neighbor. The branchless side could go against the living room wall, the bushy side was for decorations, and now the crowded tree in the woods had room to grow. Everett dragged their find through the snow by the trunk, and Anne Marie, who was four, clung to the upper branches and rode on her stomach, shouting, "Faster, Daddy!"

Pam, his wife, followed with an armload of pine boughs

and juniper branches. She seemed to have decided not to say anything more about the tree, which was fine with Everett.

The Jimmy was parked where the trail split off from the logging road, and Everett opened the back to throw the tools and boughs in, then roped the tree to the roof with nylon cords. Pam brushed off Anne Marie's snowsuit and buckled her in the front so she wouldn't get carsick. The smell of pine and juniper filled the car as they drove down the mountain.

"Chest*nuts* roasting on an open fire," Everett sang, in his best lounge-singer croon. "Jack *Frost* nipping at your nose." Here he reached over and nipped at Anne Marie's, and she squealed. He stopped, forgetting the words.

Pam prompted: "Yuletide carols," half-singing, shy about her voice.

"Being sung by a *choir* . . ." He reached for the high note.

That was when they saw the couple at the side of the road. Folks dressed up like Eskimos: Everett thought for a second that he had conjured them up with his song. The two of them stood in the snow, under the branches of a big lodgepole pine. The man wore a blue parka and held up a broken cross-country ski. The woman wore red gaiters over wool trousers, a man's peacoat, and a fur hat. They waved, and Everett slowed to a stop and rolled down the window.

"Nice day for a ski," he said.

"It was," the man said bitterly. He was about Everett's

height and age, not yet pushing forty, with a day or two of bristle on his chin.

"I broke a ski and we're lost—" the woman began.

"We're not lost," the man said.

"We are *completely* lost," the woman said.

She was younger than the man, with high, pink cheek-bones in the cold. Everett felt friendly and warm from the tree and the singing.

"Your car must be close," he said. "You're on the road."

"The car is on a different road," the woman said.

"Well, we'll find it," Everett said.

In the rearview mirror, he saw Pam's eyes widen at him from the back seat. She was slight and dark-haired, and accused him of favoring the kind of blonde who held soror-ity car washes. It was a joke, but it was partly true. With a bucket and sponge this girl would fit right in. But arguing over giving them a ride would make everyone uncomfort-able, and Pam would agree in the end. Everett got out of the car and untied a nylon cord to open the back hatch. Pam had sleds and jackets in the back seat with her, and he thought she would want some separation of family and hitchhikers. She wouldn't look at him now.

"You'll have to sit with the juniper boughs," he told the couple.

"Better than freezing in a snowbank," the blonde said, climbing into the way back. Even in the wool pants, she had a sweet figure, of the car-soaping type.

"We really appreciate this," the man said.

Everett shut them all in, lashed on the skis, and tied the tree down. It made no sense for Pam to be angry. This wasn't country where you left people in the snow. The man looked strong but not too strong; Everett could take him, if he needed to. Back in the driver's seat, Everett pulled onto the road, as snow fell in clumps off the big pine the couple had stood under.

His daughter turned around in her seat, as well as she could with her seat belt on, and announced to the new passengers, "We have a CB radio."

The warning tone in her voice came straight from Pam. It was identical in some technical, musical way to Pam's *We're going to be late,* and her *I'm not going to tell you again.*

"What's your handle?" the man in the parka asked.

Anne Marie looked confused.

"Your name," Everett explained. "On the radio."

"Batgirl," Anne Marie told the strangers, her cheeks flushing. Oh, he loved Anne Marie! Loved it when she blushed. There had been a rocky time when Pam was pregnant, when he had felt panicked and young and trapped, and slept with the wife of a friend. It had only been once, in 1974, after many beers at a co-ed softball game on the Fourth of July, but the girl had gone and told Pam. She said she needed to clear her conscience, which didn't make any sense to Everett. He'd ended up driving Pam to the emergency room after a screaming fight, when she threw a shoe at him and started to have shooting pains in her abdomen. The doctors were worried: Pam was anemic, and if she lost the baby she might bleed to death. Everett spent the night in her hospital room, frozen with grief. The baby decided to stay put, and came along fine two months later, but the night in the hospital had scared him. He would never put his wife and child in danger again. He hadn't put them in danger now, and he resented Pam's eye-widened implication that he had.

"You got a handle?" he asked the hitchhikers in back.

"I'm Clyde," the man said.

"Bonnie," the woman said.

Everyone was silent for a moment.

"That's really funny," Everett finally said—though between his shoulder blades he felt a prick of worry. "You must have a CB, too."

"No, those are our names," the man said.

The CB crackled on. "What's this 'Continental Divide'?" a man's voice asked.

Everett picked up the handset, still thinking about Bonnie and Clyde. "You mean, what is it?"

"Yeah," the voice said.

So Everett said that the snow and rain on the west side of the mountains ran to the Pacific, and the water on the east side ran to the Gulf of Mexico.

"I never heard of such a thing," the voice said.

"That's what it is," Everett said. He thought of something, the recruiting of a witness. "We just picked up some hitchhikers named Bonnie and Clyde," he said. "How about that?"

A wheezing laugh came over the radio. "No kidding?" the voice asked. "You watch your back, then. So long."

Everett hung up the handset. "So," he said to his passengers, as if he hadn't just acted out of fear of them. "Where's your stolen jalopy?"

"We parked by Fire Creek."

"You didn't get far."

"No," Bonnie said.

"How'd you break the ski?"

Bonnie and Clyde both fell silent.

Everett drove. The windows were iced from everyone's breathing, and he turned up the defrost. The fan seemed very loud. He took the road to Fire Creek, which was unpaved under the packed snow.

"This is it," he said, stopping the Jimmy.

There was a place at the trailhead to park cars, but there were no cars. Just snow and trees, and the creek running under the ice. Everett didn't look at his wife. He scanned the empty turnout and hoped this was not one of those times you look back on and wish you had done one thing different, though it had seemed perfectly natural to do what you did at the time.

"Where's the car?" Bonnie asked.

"This is where we parked," Clyde said.

They were genuinely surprised, and Everett almost

laughed with relief. There was no con, no ambush. He untied the rope, and the couple climbed out and walked to where their car had been. The girl's arm brushed against Everett's when she passed, but he didn't think she meant it. She was thinking about the missing car. He got in the Jimmy to let them discuss it. Pam reached into the way back to pull the saw and the ax from under the boughs Clyde and Bonnie had been sitting on, and she tucked the tools under her feet.

"What are we doing with these people in our car?" she asked.

"Can't leave people in the snow."

"We have a child, Everett."

"And," he said, with the confidence he had just now recovered, "we're showing her that you don't leave people in the snow. Right, Anne Marie?"

"Right," Anne Marie said, but she watched them both.

Pam gave Everett a dark, unforgiving stare. He turned back in his seat and looked out the windshield at the arguing hitchhikers. The girl, Bonnie, stamped her foot on the ground, her bare hands in fists. He liked the peacoat and fur hat combination a lot. He guessed Pam knew that. But he didn't like to be glowered at.

"I just worry," he said, trying to adopt a musing tone, "that someday I could roll all your things into a ditch, or take up with your sister, and you wouldn't have any looks left to give me. You'd have used them all up."

Pam said nothing, but looked out the window.

Everett had once argued that his affair—if one drunken night could be called that—had saved their marriage. He had thought he wanted out, but he had seen that he was wrong, and had come back for good. Pam had not been convinced by that argument. The girl he'd slept with still gave him looks at parties, looks that suggested things might start up again. Even in her confessional fit, she hadn't felt compelled to tell her husband what had happened, but Everett avoided him anyway, and the friendship had died.

Outside in the snow, Bonnie and Clyde's voices rose a notch.

"You said we could leave the keys in it!" Bonnie said. "You said this was Montana, and that's what people do!"

"That *is* what they do," Clyde said.

"Then who the *fuck* stole our car?"

Snow off the trees drifted around them, and the two stood staring at each other for a minute, then Bonnie started to laugh. She had a throaty, movie-star laugh that rose into a series of uncontrolled giggles. Her husband shook his head at her in exasperation. Everett felt the opposite; he liked her even more. A woman who could laugh at her own stolen car, and who looked like that when she did it. She was still laughing when they started back to the car.

"*You* ask for a ride," she told her husband, her voice not lowered enough.

Everett looked to Pam in the back seat; Pam frowned,

then nodded. He got out of the Jimmy, and this time the girl did brush his arm on purpose, he was sure of it. When she and Clyde were bundled in the way back again, with the tree tied down, Everett called in the theft of the car on the CB.

"Do you think we should wait for the cops?" Clyde asked.

"*I'm* not waiting in the cold anymore," Bonnie said. "Jesus, who steals a car at Christmas?"

"People do all kinds of things at Christmas," Clyde said. No one had any response to that.

The road was empty and the sky was clear. Barbed-wire fences ran evenly beside the road, and the wooden posts ticked past as they drove. In the snowy fields beyond, yellow winter grass showed through in patches. Everett peered up through the windshield at the tip of the tree, which seemed stable on the roof. He wondered if Pam could ever laugh off a stolen car. He wondered if he could. Years ago, when Pam was still in school and they were broke, they had been evicted from an attic apartment near the train yard, with nowhere to go. They had gone out for burgers to celebrate their escape from the noisy, smelly trains. He couldn't see them doing that now.

"Let's sing a song," Anne Marie said.

"Dash-ing through the snow," Everett began, and Bonnie joined in from the way back. But then Everett caught Pam's look in the mirror and stopped singing, and Anne Marie trailed out in shyness. Bonnie gamely finished, "laugh-ing all the way," in a clear voice, and then she stopped, too. Everett looked for antelope in the snow. The fenceposts ticked past.

After a while, Bonnie asked, "What will you do with the boughs?"

"Make wreaths," Pam said.

"I hope we're not crushing them."

"No."

The two women settled back into a silence just hostile enough that Everett could feel it. There didn't seem to be any antelope. There were hundreds in summer. The white-capped mountains in the east, beyond the low yellow hills, were lit up by the late sun through the clouds, and he was about to point them out to Anne Marie.

"I broke the ski," Bonnie said, out of the blue.

Everett had forgotten he had asked.

"I was cold," she said, "so we tried to take a shortcut through some fallen trees with snow on them. Clyde took his skis off, but the snow was deep and I tried to go over the logs. And the ski snapped right in half. Clyde, I'm so fucking sorry."

"Bonnie, the kid," he said.

"Sorry," she said. "But Clyde, I am."

"I know."

The sunlight had faded on the mountains again, and Everett watched the road.

"He came up here to find himself," Bonnie said. "From

Arizona, where we live, and he met this woman. She reminds me of you, actually."

Pam glanced at the woman in surprise.

"You're totally his type," Bonnie said.

"Bonnie," Clyde said.

There was a long pause, and Everett wondered what Pam was thinking, if she was at all stirred by that.

"Anyway," Bonnie went on, "she skis, and dives into glacial lakes, and canoes through rapids and what doesn't she do. And he writes me and says the air is so high and clear up here that he understands everything, and he's met his soul mate."

"Bonnie, shut up," Clyde said.

"But we're married," Bonnie said, like she was telling a funny joke. "And have a child. So I have this crazy feeling that *I'm* supposed to be his soul mate. So I leave our son with my parents and come up here, too. And we go to a party where people get naked in a hot tub and roll around in the snow. And I meet the woman, his perfect woman, and the first thing she does is proposition me."

Everett glanced at his daughter, to see what she understood. He couldn't tell. She was looking straight out the windshield. She'd seen people naked in hot tubs, so she'd understand that. He looked back at the road.

"So I told Clyde about it," Bonnie said, "thinking he'd defend my honor. And he said it was a good idea. He thought we might just move into his soul mate's cabin and get along." She seemed to think about this for a second, about the right way to sum it up. "So we tried to go for a mind-clearing ski," she said finally, "and the karmic gods stole our fucking car." She started to laugh again, the throaty start and then the giggle.

No one answered her; the only sound was her trying to stop laughing. Everett pulled quickly to the center of the road to miss a strip of black rubber truck tire.

The CB crackled on. "Continental Divide?" a voice asked.

Everett answered that he was there.

"You been shot full of bullet holes?" the man asked.

"Nope," Everett said.

"That you reporting a stolen car?"

"Have you seen it?"

"Yeah," the voice said. "I just seen Baby Face Nelson drivin' it down the road. Ha. No, I ain't seen it. I'll keep a eye out."

Everett thanked him and replaced the receiver.

"Why did he say Baby Face?" Anne Marie asked.

"There was a Bonnie and Clyde," Everett told her, "not these ones, who were bank robbers. And Baby Face Nelson was a bank robber. But he didn't like to be called Baby Face."

In the back, Bonnie said, "My first mistake was marrying someone named Clyde."

"I don't recall you being real reluctant," Clyde said.

"Do you have to talk about this *here*?" Pam burst out, and Everett was surprised. It wasn't like Pam to burst out, especially in front of strangers.

"We have to talk about it sometime," the woman said. "We were supposed to be talking up here. Then we got lost and I broke the ski and Clyde goes apeshit—"

"I did not go apeshit."

"You did," Bonnie said. "Because I'm not good at things like that. And we're ruining our son's life. These are the years that matter, he's three."

"I'm four," Anne Marie said.

Everett rumpled his daughter's hair. His wife was glaring out the window, with her arms crossed over her chest. He turned back to the road. Pam wouldn't speak again, he could tell. Whatever she was thinking would bubble and ferment and grow, but it wouldn't come out. Or it would come out where he least expected it, where it least made sense.

They were nearing the outskirts of town, the first houses. A few had decorations out: Santas and snowmen. Windows were already lit with red and green outlines, in the dim afternoon.

"Should I take you to the police station?" Everett asked, because he didn't know what else to say.

"That would be great," Clyde said.

"I'm sorry," Bonnie said. "This has been a hard time."

There was a long silence.

"What's the little girl's name?" Bonnie asked.

His daughter turned in her seat belt. "Anne Marie."

"Do you have ornaments for the tree?" Bonnie asked her.

"Yes," Anne Marie said.

"What kind?"

"Angels, and two mice sleeping in a nutshell," she said. "And some fish. And a baby Jesus in a crib."

"Those sound nice," Bonnie said, her voice wistful. "We've never had a tree. Clyde thinks you shouldn't cut down trees to put in your house."

"Bonnie," Clyde said.

Anne Marie said, "Our tree was crowding up another tree. So we made the other tree have room."

"Would that meet your standards, Clyde?" Bonnie asked.

Clyde said nothing.

Anne Marie looked out the windshield again, trained in the prevention of car sickness. "They could help decorate *our* tree," she said.

"I think they want to find their car," Everett said.

Anne Marie turned back in her seat. "Do you want to help decorate our tree?"

"Honey, they're busy," Pam said.

"I would love that more than anything in the world," Bonnie said.

"No," her husband said.

"Baby, please," Bonnie said. "We've never had a tree."

"Leave these people alone," Clyde said.

Everett turned on Broadway and stopped at the police station. He untied the rope and opened the back of the Jimmy for his passengers. Clyde didn't get out right away. He said, in a low voice, to Pam, "Look, I'm really sorry about this. Thank you for the ride." Then he climbed out, past Everett, and walked with what seemed like dignity into the station.

Bonnie sat on the boughs with her legs straight out, and gave Everett a forlorn look. In her fur hat, she looked like a Russian doll. She didn't say anything, as if she knew that silence was better, that it was what he was used to. Pam had leaned forward and was talking quietly to Anne Marie in the front seat.

"Why don't you go make your report," Everett told Bonnie. "See what they can do. I'll go home and unload, and then come back and get you both."

Two things happened at once, as in a movie, one close up and one in deep focus. Bonnie broke into a brilliant, tear-sparkled smile, and Pam's leaning form stiffened, and she half turned her head. Then she looked away again, and occupied herself more fiercely with Anne Marie. Bonnie clambered out of the back and kissed the side of Everett's mouth for a long second. "Thank you," she said.

Embarrassed, Everett stepped back and unlashed the skis and poles from the roof. He gave them to Bonnie, and she stood with the spiky bundle in her arms as they pulled away.

Pam said nothing as they drove. Their daughter must have felt the tension in the air. Everett whistled "Chestnuts roasting on an open fire," for lack of anything more sensible to do.

At the house, he parked the Jimmy and started untying the tree. Pam pulled the boughs out of the back, dumped them on the front deck, and took Anne Marie inside. Everett carried the tree around to the sliding glass door and tugged on the handle. The door didn't open. He thought it might be frozen and he tugged again. They never locked the doors. He went around the corner of the deck and pulled on the other sliding glass door, the one to the kitchen. It was locked, too. He rapped on the glass, and Pam came to it.

"The door's locked," he said, pointing to the handle.

"Say you're not going back for them," she said, her voice muffled by the glass.

The tree was heavy on his shoulder, and he stood it up on the deck, holding the slender trunk through the branches. He studied it. It was a fine tree. He turned back to his wife. "It's Christmas," he said.

"I don't want them here," she said through the glass. "Say you won't go."

"Did you lock all the doors?"

"Say it," she said.

He sighed. The temperature had dropped when the sun went down, and it was cold outside. "I won't go back for them," he said. "I'll leave them stranded and unhappy, without a tree, at Christmastime. Are you happy?"

"They're crazy," she said.

"Of course they are. Now let me in."

She unlocked the door. He carried the tree through the kitchen, set it up in the corner of the living room, and turned it until the bare side faced the wall. It looked like a lopsided bush. Anne Marie clapped her hands in approval. He showed her how to fill the reservoir in the stand with water. Then he crumpled newspaper in the fireplace, built a hut of kindling, and set it alight.

Pam called the police station to renege on the hospitality, asking them to deliver the message to the people whose car was stolen. Everett strung the lights on the tree, and lifted Anne Marie to put the angel on top. There wasn't really a single top to the tree, but he helped her pick one. Pam moved around the kitchen, making dinner.

A stranger watching would have thought it a perfectly ordinary December night, and it was true that they talked no more than they often did. Anne Marie gamely kept up an almost professional patter, like a hostess who knows her party has gone wrong and her guests are miserable. She hung the ornaments: the two mice sleeping in the nutshell, the fish, the baby Jesus in the crib. Everett sat in the big chair between the fireplace and the kitchen, feeling the soreness from chopping and hauling set in. He wasn't twenty-five anymore.

Anne Marie sang Christmas carols to herself: "It Came Upon a Midnight Clear" and "Good King Wenceslas."

With a pot of soup on the stove, Pam made a juniper swag for the mantelpiece, her slimness in jeans set off by the firelight. She cut and arranged the boughs as she had every year they had been in the house, and as her mother had every year before that. She nestled three white candles among the branches, evenly spaced, and lit them. Everett watched her, thinking about the fact that she was Clyde's type, wondering why he still wanted to go get the outlaws, and put himself in the way of temptation.

Pam turned from the mantel with the matchbook. There was sometimes a funny, ironic smile that came over her face when she caught him looking at her, a grown-up smile, at once confident and self-deprecating. But now she looked defiant and young. It was the look Anne Marie got at bedtime, when made to choose how to spend her dwindling time: this book or that book? Staying up by the fire or having ten minutes more with her dolls? Anne Marie always delayed and evaded, and chose the longest book, the most involved game.

Pam said, "Look, if you want to go get them, just go."

"They'll have gone by now," he said, with a catch in his voice.

Pam threw the burnt match into the fire, and put the matchbook in the kitchen drawer. Then she picked up and dialed the phone, watching Everett, as if waiting for him to stop her.

"I called earlier about the couple with the stolen car," she said, in her businesslike phone voice. "Are they still there?" She waited, looking out the dark glass door she had locked him out of.

"Hi, Bonnie," she said into the phone. "It's Pam—from the car. We picked you up. Hi." Her laugh sounded social, but Everett could hear the nervousness in it. "No, I don't think I introduced myself. Do you still want to help with the tree? Everett could run down and get you."

She paused, listening.

"Put Clyde on," she said, and she turned away from Everett. He watched the curve of his wife's ass as she leaned on the kitchen counter, lifting her right foot and nervously tapping the toe on the floor. "Clyde," she said. "Please come up for dinner. Anne Marie would love to show off the tree." The pause again. "Really, we'd love it," she said. Then, "Good. He'll be right down."

She hung up the phone, and turned to Everett. "Merry Christmas," she said.

He was not sure how to behave. Anne Marie was still decorating the lower branches of the tree, singing, "We three kings of orien-tare." There were plenty of branches left for Bonnie.

"So," Pam said. She stirred the pot on the stove with a

wooden spoon, tapped the spoon against the rim, and set it on the counter. "Do you want to go get them?"

Everett pushed himself out of the chair. "Want to come along, Anne Marie?" he asked.

His daughter looked up at him. "Are you going to get those people?"

"Yes," he said. "To help with the tree."

Anne Marie nodded, untangling the loop of string on a tiny ukulele. "I'll stay here," she said.

He kissed Pam goodbye on the top of her head. Was she attracted to Clyde? He wanted to take off her clothes right now and see. He was conscious of his own breathing, and he could tell she was unsteady.

"It's Christmastime," he said. "I'll be right back."

He went out into the cold air. The Jimmy started up easy, and he headed in low gear down the hill toward town.

He wanted to decide, as he drove, what they were doing. He wanted to separate his impulse to be a good Samaritan from the kiss on the corner of his mouth. Bonnie did not, he was fairly sure, just want to hang angels on a tree. Clyde's asking her to move in with his mistress had put her in a giddy, reckless mood, and Everett was the beneficiary. He wasn't going to think about Clyde's low, sincere apology to Pam. Or about Pam turning away on the phone to ask Clyde to come to the house. Although he found he wanted very much to think about that.

He thought instead about Anne Marie, and how the

evening might work out for her. The lesson about not abandoning people was a good one. The silent, submerged unhappiness of the evening couldn't be good for a kid, and now it was gone, dissolved by Pam's call into the buzz of unsettled excitement.

The streets were dark and empty, the houses warm with light. He wanted to keep thinking, but he was at the station before he had sorted things out, and Bonnie was waiting on the curb. She climbed into the front seat and kicked the snow off her boots.

"Hi," she said, and she clutched her hands in her lap. She shuddered once, from nervousness or cold. "Clyde'll be here in a second," she said. "He's signing something about the car."

"Okay," he said.

She looked at Everett and seemed about to say something, and then she was in his arms. He gathered her up as well as he could, given her thick coat and the awkward position, and kissed her sweet face. Her cheeks were cold but her lips were warm, and she was trembling. The peacoat was unbuttoned, and he reached inside to feel the curve of her breast through her sweater.

A second later they pulled apart—the time required to sign papers measured somewhere in both their minds—and Bonnie smoothed her hair. The lighted glass door of the station opened, and Clyde walked with his long stride toward them and got in the back seat.

Everett thought there must be a smell in the car from the kiss, an electricity. But the husband said nothing, and Everett drove the outlaws back to his house. They talked about the stolen car, and the cold, and the tree. All the while, Everett felt both the threat of disorder and the steady, thrumming promise of having everything he wanted, all at once.

ABOUT THE AUTHOR

Maile Meloy is the author of the story collection *Half in Love*, and the novels *Liars and Saints* and *A Family Daughter*. Meloy's stories have been published in *The New Yorker, Granta, Zoetrope: All-Story*, and other publications. She has been shortlisted for the UK's Orange Prize, and has received *The Paris Review*'s Aga Khan Prize for Fiction, the PEN/ Malamud Award, the Rosenthal Foundation Award from the American Academy of Arts and Letters, and a Guggenheim Fellowship. In 2007, she was chosen as one of *Granta*'s Best Young American Novelists. She lives in Los Angeles.

A NOTE ON TYPE

The text of this book was set in Bembo,
based on a roman cut by
Francesco Griffo
in Venice in 1945.

This book was designed by
Amanda Dewey.

This book was printed and bound
by R. R. Donnelly
in Bloomsburg, Pennsylvania.